A Reluctant Warrior

A Novel
about
Manuel Velasquez

First printing, September 2008

This novel is a work of fiction, though some of the
characters and scenes were inspired by a few interviews
with Manuel Velasquez and his wife and by additional
research. Characters and places are either the products
of the author's imagination or used fictitiously.

Any resemblance to actual persons living or dead
is entirely coincidental.

ISBN 978-0-6152-5159-2
Published by Phyllis Owens, assisted by AllawayBooks
www.allawaybooks.com

Printed by Lulu in the United States of America
www.lulu.com

Acknowledgements

With affection and gratitude I thank my family for their unwavering encouragement and support. A special thanks to my late husband Tom, who lovingly encouraged me in my dreams and endeavors.

For many years I worked in the legal profession and always thought I may write one day. It has been so interesting that every member of my family encouraged me and gave me ideas when I was not sure how to move forward. The grandchildren were also helpful, even the younger ones. They were eager to offer ideas and unfailing enthusiasm.

My Family: Daughter Teresa Briggs and her son Christopher Briggs; Son Richard Owens, daughter-in-law Barbara and their children Samantha and Stephen; Daughter Sherry Fortner and her daughter McKenna Fortner.

Sincere thanks to my friends: Audrey Masters, an artist, who not only helped and encouraged me, but also painted the cover. She can be reached at 509-575-1925. To Roberta Champoux for her ongoing patience and encouragement; Gwyn Makowichuk for her encouragement and help in proof reading; also Frank Orozco who offered help regarding folk lore and customs.

Al Allaway, author and publisher who prepared format and submitted the book for printing.

"Kick Start Divas,"... my writing group members who critiqued some of the drafts offering sage advice and encouragement: Miriam Avlon, Betty Bennett, Judy Brandt, Sharon French, Jan Mosbrucker and Nancy Spracher.

Special thanks and appreciation to Wendy Warren, my friend and accomplished writing coach, who offered ongoing encouragement and patiently critiqued most of the manuscript. Wendy is our mentor at *"Kick Start Divas."* She can be contacted at www.wendywarren.org or wendy@wendywarren.org

Manuel Velazquez

A Reluctant Warrior

By Phyllis Owens

Chapter 1

I could never have imagined that my life would be so rich with passion and the love of more than one beautiful woman, or that from such meager beginnings I would have an incredibly exciting life. I was coerced and very well trained by the Mexican government in Mexico City as an undercover agent. My story spans a tumultuous history. The massacre in 1968 at Tlatelolcok Plaza nearly cost me my life. Later I became known as one of the best drivers for high-speed chases and later still was a personal bodyguard to the El Presidente of Mexico. But I'm getting ahead of my story.

In Mexico City, on December 24th, 1950, I came into this world born to a mother who was unhappy, overworked, and trying to make a marriage work. I was

given the name of Manuel Velasquez. My
father was a peaceful kind man who loved
us; he just didn't accept his responsibilities. He worked now and then and
drank too much. Three other children were
born after me. My sister Marcella was born
and then two brothers Saul and Renee. We
all played together, loved each other and
remained close. We had such fun, the little
toddlers giggling when I swung them and
played like we were all puppies whining
and yipping.

My father Bernardo, was handsome,
always sported a large moustache and
smelled faintly of lime which maybe he
rubbed on his clothes or person. I don't
think they could afford things like after-
shave. He was weathered and wrinkled by
working outside as a gardener. He did care
about us but really was no match for
mother's temperament.

My mother was a very pretty woman,
fine boned and slender and dressed often
in skirts and blouses in bright colors. Her
eyes were jet black and almost sparked
when she was mad. Her grandparents
were French and her complexion, though
her hair was black, was fairer than most
Mexicans. She adored jewelry and
treasured every piece she was able to save

up and purchase or pieces she received as gifts

She was lightning quick to anger and doled out hurtful discipline to us children on the spot. We were not doing bad things, just being normal children. But mother had no patience whatsoever with we children. She didn't have much patience with father either. She would yell at him that he was useless and kicked him out completely whenever she couldn't abide his drinking, or if he was not working steady and, of course, if he didn't agree with her on the politics of the day.

We lived in a small very modest, battered looking adobe house on the outskirts of Mexico City in a very ordinary neighborhood. The inside of our house was crowded, we three boys had to sleep in the same bed and our sister had a small cot in a room off the hall that wasn't really a bedroom, just a small room a little bigger than a closet. Mom tried to keep our home tidy and fought the accumulation of constant clutter, but that was a job in and of itself, especially with all of us to deal with.

Our yard was full of pieces and ends of lumber, car parts, broken bikes and toys and a couple of crooked chairs that were our lawn furniture. Bright pink, purple and white bougainvillea crawled across fences from one yard to another and up tree trunks and poles giving the tired neighborhood a riot of beautiful color. The houses were built rather close together. In most yards a few kinds of cacti were cultivated and when in bloom smelled sweet in the night air. The streets were not paved so dust hung in the still air and was a common annoyance.

There was a bus stop two blocks away and most people used the bus service, as automobiles were a luxury. The bus was very warm and slow, made so many stops and yes, at times there were people carrying a chicken or a small goat or rabbit. Of course, there were young children perpetually whining, complaining but paying no attention to their parent's scolding. Bicycles were widely utilized for transportation because sometimes it was faster than the bus if the destination was not too far away.

Since I was the oldest, my mother poured responsibility on me, partly, I guess because my father did not accept those responsibilities. Also I was taller and stockier than most boys my age so maybe she expected more of me without thinking of my youth. I believe that I always wanted my mother's approval, but it was never bestowed on me. I was expected to help at home with cooking, cleaning house, washing and diapering the babies. I watched the children and took care of them for long periods of time while my mother had to go outside the home to work.

One day she came home and I had not done my chores to her satisfaction. She immediately got a wrestler's grip around my neck, drug me out to a large tree in the front yard, tied a rope around my feet and with help she enlisted from my siblings, hoisted me and hung me upside down from a large limb. She then beat me repeatedly with a belt and left me there. She hollered at my sister and brothers to go with her and they walked down the two blocks, got on the bus and went to town.

It is very hot in Mexico City and my feet and legs hurt very badly and I was crushed that my mother would treat me so badly. I had been taking care of the little children all day. As I hung there upside down, my heart was heavy realizing the extent of my mother's wrath. I did not feel I was deserving of such treatment. I was used to her tirades and beatings with sticks, belts or whatever she could grab but this new torture was so much worse. My head was pounding and I felt faint and after what seemed like forever, a neighbor finally heard my cries and came and got me down. He said I looked almost black. I was ill for the rest of the day. My mother never asked me how I got down. Everything went on normally at home as if the incident never happened.

We kids always had a good time and played whenever we could. The neighborhood kids would all get together and play in a vacant lot or in someone's yard. We played ball, hide and seek, built things in the dirt and rode bikes when we had one that worked.

One thing we boys always enjoyed was fighting, when we were like five or six. When we were younger, it would be over a toy unshared or an insult or push or shove we thought was a jab to fight. Later the fights were over a girlfriend or one we wanted to be our girlfriend and maybe she was paying attention to one of the other guys. We must have thought we would show her how much we really cared, trying to impress her with our fearless haste to battle. This quickness to fight must be in our genes. We would fight also if we thought we had been insulted or wronged. If we played soccer and thought someone took an unfair jab at us or tripped us, anything like that would set us off. We usually hit and wrestled and rolled on the ground, really never hurt each other badly.

One family had a couple pair of old boxing gloves and they let us use them. We staged organized matches out in a field a couple blocks from our house. My best friend Felix was a thin, short guy and tough as nails. He was so fast he would hit his opponent before they even knew what happened. Even though we would all fight at the drop of a hat, we were still friends after.

One day soon after the hanging incident, my mother came home and announced to me that I either had to improve my attendance at school and get better grades or take a job she had found me in a furniture factory close by. Interestingly, my missing school was due to her having me stay home and take care of the little ones while she had to work. I didn't say anything to her about that. My grades were average. I loved my art classes and did well in those, but the prospect of learning a trade appealed to me. I announced I would take the job at the furniture factory. My age was twelve at the time.

Mother evidently talked grandma into coming over and watching the smaller children during the day. They were a bit older by now and out of diapers so Grandma managed pretty well. She was also of a sweeter temperament.

The prospect of getting out and learning something new was very exciting for me. I loved the wood, metals and materials we used. The men working were helpful and I was able to learn much about hand building furniture, carving, assembling and varnishing and painting. We also made wrought iron and metal furniture, which I seemed to have a natural talent for. We welded these so I learned about welding also. There were a couple of other young guys my age working there, Juan and Arturo, and we became fast friends. We laughed and sang and joked and got together whenever we could on our days off.

When I started becoming a young man about 13, girls in the neighborhood fascinated me and I could scarcely think of anything else. They would flirt, tease and torment me. A girl in a low cut blouse or bare legs when the girls wore shorts would unnerve me at once.

A bunch of us neighborhood kids went down by the river where there was underbrush and a few trees for cover. We would all bring a little soda (or beer if we were that lucky), a snack of some kind and share what we all had, even as meager as it sometimes was. We skinny-dipped and chased each other all around, playing tag and tumble. We never tired of this activity. Towards nightfall, we explored each other's bodies, giggled and laughed and figured out what all the hushed, never mentioned taboo subject of sex was all about. Interestingly, the girls were just as excited about all this as we boys.

These activities escalated over that year. We'd all run for home as soon as dark fell knowing we'd be in big trouble if we were late for dinner and in some cases in time to help with dinner.

I remember that when my girlfriend, Sylvia, looked into my eyes and flirted with me, my heart would pound and the blood would rush to my head and I would be instantly and completely aroused. I became sexually active at age 14. In my culture at that time, we had sex parties like orgies and shared sexual partners on a regular basis.

Manual at a young age (center).

Chapter 2

One day as I walked along on my way home from work at the furniture factory, I noticed a beautiful girl standing in the doorway of a shoe store, her figure full and her glance inviting. I stopped and visited with her every day after work. Her name was Delores. She was a vision with long beautiful hair, voluptuous body, and she was easy to talk to and seemed to care a lot for me. We shared sodas and talked and then I would head home after the day cooled off a bit. We spent as much time as we could together and made out a lot.

Neither of us was very happy at home and we enjoyed each other so much that after only a few months, we decided to get married. We knew it was a wild and crazy idea and I didn't even want to ask my parents' permission since I was just 15, so I falsified a birth certificate and said I was 18. Delores was 19 at the time. My mother was furious, but my father seemed to have some understanding of my feelings, although he knew I was way too young for marriage. Her family was not aware of my age.

Delores's parents were nice people. Her father worked at the newspaper, where he set type. Her mother did not work outside the home although she did some childcare. Delores had only one sister a couple years younger than she who still attended high school. They lived in a pleasant neighborhood in a big older adobe home that sat on a corner lot. They had painted the house a soft light blue-green, like a robin's egg. Lucy, her mother, loved to garden and flowers bloomed here and there all the time. It was a cheerful house with all the colors of the flowers and plantings. It was easy to find in the neighborhood. Homes in that area were painted pastel colors but none the shade of theirs.

I got along well with them, although I knew they thought I was older than I really was. They loved to play cards and I had played cards with my dad enough to understand the games so they were happy to have us stay at home with them and play.

We did get married. I loved Delores passionately and completely and she returned my feelings. I gave up my occasional promiscuous sex parties and tried to be a good husband. Our time together was enjoyable; we went to parks, took long walks, visited our friends and talked of the future.

We moved into a tiny apartment not far from where we both worked in a neighborhood fairly close to the business district. It was actually the wing of a larger house that had been made into an apartment. We didn't have much furniture at first. Delores's family had a couple things they gave us, a small table with a little leaf that slid out at mealtime and was put back after. It had two chairs with it. My aunt and uncle were kind enough to give us a brown vinyl couch when they got a new one. My grandma gave us a bed and mattress so we really managed quite well. The kitchen was on one short wall of the small living room. Delores and her mother painted the whole apartment a light turquoise. That was a good light bright color for the space.

There was just one small bedroom and it was so narrow, we fit the bed and mattress in and to get out of my side of the bed, I had to get out at the foot of the bed. Delores had only a few feet of room on her side. We got the giggles sometimes when I stood up and walked down the bed and stepped off the end.

A little bathroom with just a shower was located off of our bedroom. We shared one closet in the bedroom and most of my things were stacked neatly in a couple boxes in the bedroom. We managed just fine though and Delores had a great disposition, never complained.

I left the furniture factory because I was offered a full time job at a garage near our apartment. Growing up, I had helped the neighbor boys work on their cars, also helped some of the neighbors and had a little mechanical background. Mr. Alfonso who owned the garage agreed to teach me to be a mechanic. The pay was better and I had a chance to learn another trade. He was a pleasant man and a fair one. He expected a day's work for a day's pay. I made sure to work hard and always offered to help him finish for the day, even if it was after the hours I would be paid for. Learning a new trade was exciting for me and I liked it.

I saw my uncle when he brought his car to the garage. He would give me updates on my family, as I didn't see them often. My aunt and uncle were kind to me and probably knew what a tough child-hood I endured to that point. They invited

Delores and I over for dinner and we always enjoyed those evenings.

After our marriage, my mother discouraged my siblings from keeping in contact with me, although when they had a chance, they wrote. My father stopped by the garage from time to time and encouraged me to keep learning.

Delores was a good wife and marriage agreed with me. She had a healthy sexual appetite and became pregnant in the first year of our marriage. We were excited about the prospect of having our own child. I was concerned about the size of our apartment, but babies are little so we figured we could look for a larger place when it became necessary.

Money concerns plagued me; I was just a kid unable to make a decent wage. Despite that, things went all right until Delores was unable to work the last two months of pregnancy. Her doctor said she needed to be off her feet, but that she would probably be fine.

The reality of every day married life and responsibilities of marriage were becoming clear to us. The unfortunate reality of this union was that I had trouble supporting us. When Delores couldn't work in the last two months of her pregnancy, we didn't even have enough food to eat. My feelings of inadequacy and shame were with me all the time.

After a difficult labor with Delores's mother and a midwife assisting, our baby was stillborn. We were devastated. I felt so awful for Delores. We thought maybe the lack of nutritious food during her pregnancy caused the problem with the baby. We tried to settle back into normal living but were both distraught about losing the baby.

Her parents were good and came and helped me comfort Delores and take care of her. They were counting on their first grandchild, however, and were also mourning that loss.

I went to the church in town to make burial arrangements for our baby boy and since I hadn't the price of burial, they refused me. My grief was heavy, but knowing that I had to go home and tell Delores this news was hideous. I went home and built a little box, put our son in it and carried him on my back to the next town where they had a pauper's graveyard and they took care of the burial.

By this time the stress and our circumstances had taken a toll on our marriage. Delores worked more and I felt she withdrew from me and I couldn't blame her. Finally the next year, things improved slightly and Delores became pregnant. We did everything we could to see that she ate as healthy as possible and she delivered a bouncing baby boy. We named him Johnnie. He was a darling baby and we were happy. She was a wonderful, caring mother and she even seemed happier with me once again.

The financial problems were still great however, and things deteriorated. Delores couldn't work the hours she had before. Her mother tried to help with the baby, but she couldn't do much as she had her own childcare business at home. They didn't live that close either so getting Johnnie back and forth was difficult, as we didn't have a car. We walked to work and took the bus if we needed transportation.

I missed my art studies and started thinking about taking some night courses at the college nearby. I hoped I could sell some things to earn extra money. I had always been artistic and did a lot of drawing and some oil painting and also had the metal and wood working background from the furniture factory.

Delores encouraged me and I enrolled. Classes began a month later. I took water color, drawing and sculpting. My teachers told me my work was very good. I found it a little harder to spend time with Delores and Johnnie but things were going all right.

Learning and practicing every spare minute at college helped me become proficient at sculpting, painting and metal art. I had done both oil and watercolor pictures and had a small showing with two other artists at a local art exhibit and sold every one of my paintings.

I worked on my art projects diligently and learned all I could from the teachers. I felt I was meant to be an artist.

One large project I was asked to help with was a series of very large murals that were to be painted on the outside of different buildings in a slum neighborhood, to improve the appearance and uplift the residents.

The artist who was commissioned to oversee all the details of this project was an inspiration to me. He explained his techniques to me, shared methods of mixing the colors and the use of various brushes for certain effects. Every spare minute that I wasn't working at the garage was spent helping with the murals. It was a great experience.

My art teacher called me in after the project was completed and told me that the directing artist and my art teachers all had discussed my contribution. They all agreed that I had real talent and hoped I would continue to apply myself. This advice I took to heart. One of my personal assignments that I worked on carefully was a pen dot picture, tedious work, quite large of Inca ruins, which was purchased and displayed in the lobby of one of the banks in town.

My counselor encouraged me to take other studies and get a degree. I shifted my energies to complete the required classes and get credits for them.

My studies went well and I loved college: the social aspect, the learning and the dedication of the gifted and helpful teachers.

Everything went well. I was able to keep up things at home, although Delores was still a bit withdrawn from me and I secretly thought she enjoyed the time I was away. My ego suffered because of this. Work at the garage was going good, and I was on my way to obtaining my degree.

Chapter 3

However, trouble was waiting for me in the campus coffee shop one evening. Occasionally I grabbed a bite after my evening classes. Looking for a place to sit after getting my sandwich and coffee, I walked past a table and a very attractive young lady said, "Here, there's a chair by me. You're more than welcome to sit here."

I said, "Thank you very much," and joined her. We visited and the time flew. Before we knew it, most of the customers had left the coffee shop and we were still there. Her name was Marlena and she was beautiful. She was tall and had a lovely figure and her legs were incredible. To this day, I don't think I've seen prettier legs than she had. She said, "I frequently have my dinner here at this time; I'd love to see you again soon."

I looked into her eyes and replied, "Oh, you can be sure you'll see me very soon."

Dinner hour found me most evenings at a table with Marlena. She was so easy to talk to, intelligent and her sense of humor was great. She was stunning and obviously interested in me. My guard was down. My attraction to this beautiful creature was increasing by the day. I didn't fail to tell her I was married and wore my wedding band. Despite that, our friendship turned into a romance fairly fast.

Chapter 4

After I returned home late several times, Delores figured out something was wrong and when she accused me of cheating, I confessed to her that I had met another. My feelings were mixed. I felt terrible for hurting her. I knew I was causing future pain for my son. I struggled with all this, but Delores and I had grown apart. A feeling of relief swept over me now that it was out in the open. Delores was raging mad and, of course, hurt but I held her and we cried and talked about everything and she admitted that she was not happy in our marriage either.

She was proud of me for pursuing an education but had felt I didn't care about her and that I hadn't helped her at all with Johnnie. I was young and must have been thinking of myself because I knew she was right. She told me that she wanted to move in with her parents. They loved Johnnie to pieces so I helped her pack and she and our child moved to her parents' home. I assured her I would send what money I could and that I must visit my son regularly. She agreed to visitation and told me to get divorce papers prepared pronto.

My new love, Marlena, was 16 and studying nursing at the time. I was now 19. Marlena adored me and said she was fascinated with me. I couldn't resist her charm. As soon as I had gotten a divorce from Delores, Marlena and I started planning our wedding. We were married as soon as she finished nursing training five months later. We had a pleasant little ceremony at her parents' home with just her family and our close friends present.

I was not in contact with my family at the time. There was never a way to please my mother and she found fault with everything I did in life. Unfortunately, she insisted on talking badly about me to my sister and brothers. They probably felt that if they had a close relationship with me it would be at the risk of losing their relationship with our mother, who seemed kinder and more accepting of them.

Even though I tried my whole life to figure why my mother treated me the way she did, I have never known why. Usually a first-born son has a special place in a mother's heart. For my mother, this didn't happen. It was as if my being born didn't suit her and her feelings toward me never changed. As a young boy, I tried to show my mother how much I loved her and I was so hurt by her treatment of me. I did keep in contact with my father from time to time and I feel he always loved me but never interfered in my mother's harsh treatment of me.

After our wedding, my bride and I took a weekend honeymoon to a small resort in the country and talked and dreamed of our life together. The resort was up in the hills, out of town and quiet, romantic and peaceful. I had rented the honeymoon suite and surprised Marlena. As I carried her over the threshold, she squealed happily when she saw the suite. It was large with a big comfortable bed and lots of fluffy pillows. The room was done in different shades of blue and the view from the window looked out over a stream running through a green pasture where a few cattle grazed.

There was a bucket and ice with champagne and a nice fruit plate and a couple of baskets with assorted snacks.

We were tired but I poured us each a glass of champagne and made a toast that I loved her madly and promised to be a good husband. We then took off our clothes and comfortably got between the cool sheets of the big bed. We were meant to be together and as Marlena pulled me to her and gave me a passionate kiss, it seemed the most natural thing that we make love. We were good together, our timing seemed perfect and we were in tune with each other's needs. The honeymoon was every bit as good as we had hoped.

The next morning, a tray was left outside our door with a thermos of fresh hot coffee, assorted rolls and fresh fruit. We were hungry and enjoyed the offering. Unfortunately we had to get ready to check out by three in the afternoon and drive home.

We began our life together in a cozy but small apartment. It was furnished with old things mostly, but clean and since we were newlyweds, we were just happy to be together. Marlena added her touch to the apartment and always had a vase of fresh flowers on the table and kept our place tidy. The landlord had painted it traditional Mexican colors, bright oranges, reds and yellows. The color made a shabby apartment quite pleasing to the eye.

Marlena always welcomed Johnnie into our life. When I brought him home, he ran into her open arms. She hugged him and kissed his little round cheeks. He loved the stories she read to him. Even though our place was small, there was a little courtyard with flowers climbing on a tall wooden fence. It was a great spot with evening shade. We put some old chairs and a table out there and invited people over for dinner often. She cooked meals and we served them in the courtyard.

Chapter 5

After a time, Marlena and I began talking about what we would do with our lives; did we want to live in the city or move to a village? Perhaps we should consider the country? After about a year and a half we were seriously considering other possibilities. I wanted to continue my artwork and sculpting and there just wasn't room in the little apartment.

We talked about how tired we both were of the big, dusty city and the heat so we started to consider moving somewhere else. We had heard jobs were plentiful in Acapulco. After planning and saving we visited there and it looked promising. The cooler climate and fresh air in Acapulco appealed to us.

There was a small but cozy house for rent two blocks from a lovely stretch of beach and we knew at once it was perfect. We rented the house and gave notices to our employers and set about moving in two weeks, which went smoothly. We didn't take all our furniture, deciding it was easier to purchase some used things if needed.

The kitchen was small but adequate, with a little stove and refrigerator and room for table and chairs. Walls of sunny yellow made it a light, happy room. There was a little sun porch with space for me to set up an easel and some paints and art supplies. I did my sculpting outside and locked things up in a funny little shed in back of the house. Marlena made curtains for the porch windows, blue, the color of the ocean and she found a couple of easy chairs and small desk at a second hand store for my sun porch studio. For the little living room, we had gotten a used couch and rocking chair at a consignment store.

Marlena's family brought our bed, a table and chairs and a couple of tables for the living room on a visit so we had everything we needed and settled in. Her family adored the beach and was reluctant to leave.

We spent time in this sunny paradise walking along in the sand, taking an occasional swim and then napping in the shade. Green sea turtles inhabited the waters and were always fascinating to watch. Fresh seafood was abundant. We enjoyed preparing fresh caught lobster and mahi-mahi. Being close to the ocean was good medicine for us both.

Manuel met Brooke Shields when she was vacationing in Acapulco

Marlena had studied English at her parents' insistence and was quite fluent. She was excited to teach me, and I began learning right away. I studied regularly and Marlena was a good teacher.

Once a month I rode into Mexico City with my friend Raul, who drove a truck hauling fresh seafood to the city, allowing

me visits with my son Johnnie at very little
cost. Once we arrived in the city, Raul
dropped me off at Delores's and I took
Johnnie on the bus to town. We spent the
night in a motel.

Johnnie and I had such good times
together. I began to teach him English. I
knew that it would be useful to him in life.
He seemed to enjoy it and was a fast
learner. They say children can learn
languages easily when they are very young
and it was true of Johnnie. I was proud of
him.

On the drive to and from the city,
Raul and I listened to music and talked
about our futures and life in general. For
us these topics were mainly our work,
women and politics. We laughed a lot too
and avoided politics right quick if we
disagreed on a policy or new legislation by
the government. He was glad to have
someone along to keep him company and
to drive if he got tired.

Raul was a single man and would
tease me about being tied down to a wife. I
would tell him his single life wasn't good
for him because he didn't get enough rest
and he would never have anything
because he spent his money on the women
he dated. I told him he needed to meet a

rich woman, sweep her off her feet and marry her quick. Then we'd laugh about the possibilities of that happening.

The beach at Acalpulco

Chapter 6

I had been able to land a job doing mechanic work on the metro trains in Acapulco. There was a learning curve, but soon my mechanical background made it possible for me to do the necessary repairs on the trains and equipment. The pay was good and the people I worked with were pleasant. I made friends with two of my co-workers, Roberto and Eduardo. We were all close in age, they were both married and our wives seemed to enjoy each other.

There were many picnics on the beach that we shared, sunset walks and trips on weekends to the country. We fellows got together after work for a couple beers sometimes and talked about work and life and our families. Neither of them had children yet. I didn't tell them I had a boy already by a prior marriage Secretly, although I loved children, I knew the difference they made to a marriage. Marlena and I had decided to wait to have children and enjoy each other.

My artwork reflected now the palm trees, sultry shores, beautiful sunsets as well as colorful bougainvillea, poinsettia and the other flowers of Acapulco. My paintings sold fairly well, two shops nearby let me display them on consignment. That was fair; I didn't mind paying a commission to the shopkeepers for hanging my paintings where people would notice. I sculpted dolphin and turtles out of local pale green limestone. They were two and a half feet tall. These large sculptures became popular and I sold quite a lot of them.

One of the local garden stores became a regular customer as well.

I was still working on my English and getting better at it. Marlena and I spoke English at home. Pronunciation was hard to learn, but with her help, I was making good progress. We were enjoying our life in Acapulco.

Chapter 7

After a couple years, we started hearing about the Campeche Jungle and how beautiful it was, wild and unspoiled. Books about this area told of many remarkable Mayan ruins throughout the surrounding area. We thought we could do a lot of exploring in our off hours and learn all about life in the jungle.

Newspaper articles told about job programs being offered by the government. By investigating these opportunities, Marlena and I learned the programs were offered to motivate people with various skills to move to the jungle and help educate the tribes there. They wanted teachers for the local people, especially for reading and writing and Marlena thought it sounded like a great idea. She had taken classes to teach people to read and write while we were in Acapulco and had a special talent for it.

The jungle is just north of the Mexico-Guatemala border covering almost 15% of the State of Campeche. This jungle was home to an incredible variety of trees, plants, animals and birds. The beaches were said to be beautiful and accessible.

Today, occupying the large state's eastern border with Quintana Roo State is a big track of tropical jungle, 1.5 million acres. It is all a protected reserve, the largest in Mexico.

A Nearby Village

We took a week to explore. We went into the jungle and visited the little village where desirable jobs were available. Small government houses would be furnished, though sparsely, for people like us to live in. Acreage had been cleared for farming and the local villagers seemed friendly, expressing their willingness to learn the ways of the outside world.

Two hundred miles north of the village, we also visited the state's capital, the coastal colonial town of Campeche. It was founded in 1540 on the site of a

Mayan trading village. Campeche was the Yucatan's principal colonial port, thanks to its defensive system, one of the Western Hemisphere's best. As was done in Cartagena, Columbia, a stone wall shaped like a hexagon stretches some 2.5 km surrounding the city. There are old rusty cannons down on the waterfront that once defended the port.

The old city a crumbling, interesting port filled with naval history and aged Spanish architecture, was beautiful in its individuality, a coastal gem. Just a short distance from the little town, the beaches were serene and secluded.

Campeche is a wealthy town dotted with fine mansions and civic buildings as well as museums and a beautiful old cathedral. The city's streets are nearly all cobblestone and the buildings brightly painted.

Seeing all the beauty, mystery and enchantment of the jungle helped us make up our minds. It was an opportunity that we wanted to take advantage of.

My only concern was not seeing my boy Johnnie often enough. Marlena and I agreed that our stay would not be lengthy. A couple years would no doubt be enough time to live the lifestyle required. The programs were year to year so we felt that was fair and not so confining that we couldn't handle it. We decided to take the big step, gave notice to our employers and arranged to move. Summer clothing and our personal things were all we could take. I brought a few art supplies and Marlena brought her portable sewing machine and a little fabric. Our adventure was now underway.

There were opportunities for men who could do mechanic work. The women would teach the locals how to provide more nourishing meals. I signed up for the mechanic work which involved using the tractors and farm equipment and teaching the natives to use them as well. It was understood that if any other mechanical expertise was needed in any of the other programs, I would assist.

The government homes were in a little compound next to the village. Marlena said they looked like barracks. She was right, they really did but all were clean and fairly new, small but adequate. The whole group of buildings was painted beige and had red metal roofs. The homes were furnished us as part of our incentive to move there and work.

It was exciting, meeting lots of other young people who had decided to come here too.

Moving in and getting settled didn't take us long and we were anxious to get our assignments and explore the area whenever we had time.

Marlena got busy with her sewing machine and set about making curtains. She and her sewing machine were instantly in great demand. The other newcomers asked for help with similar projects. The local women begged for help assembling dresses, aprons, skirts for themselves and clothes for the children. The visiting missionaries were asked to put the word out that the women needed fabric for all these items.

Unfortunately, no paving had been done so the area was quite dusty. Then when it rained, it was very muddy. We sent word to the government officials that paving was badly needed in our compound and the school grounds.

Despite the hardships, Marlena liked her teaching position. Two other teachers had been hired also and a nice new little school had been built. The people of the community were happy to have the new school and appreciated the teachers.

At first, however, the parents and children didn't understand the rules of school attendance. Students tended to come and go as they wished. Parents would just keep them home to help with chores and not see the importance of attending class regularly. After a teacher-parent conference, the children began attending school regularly with blessings from their parents.

Another problem was head lice. The teachers had been alerted about this problem and furnished a good supply of medicine for it. Marlena confided to me that she was surprised at the number of children who had the head lice and she got the teachers to discuss this. They all knew that unless the medicine was supplied to the parents also and the homes eradicated of the lice, the problem would not be solved.

Children also had a dysentery condition so medicine was requested from headquarters for that, as well as a lot more of the lice treatment. With regular public meetings these problems were addressed, and the children and parents both treated. They were taught about using the medicine and how to eradicate lice from their living quarters.

The dysentery medicine worked well and we ordered it regularly so there was always plenty on hand

Marlena liked her work. She and the other teachers were greatly appreciated by parents and children alike. One of the other teachers taught music to the children. They put on a little program one evening. It was like listening to little angels singing. There were a few flutes available and a few of the older children were taught to play. They accompanied the singers very nicely.

My duties were beginning, too, and I was anxious to get the crops in. The jungle encroached onto our paths and roads. I had to make sure the workers wielded their machetes often clearing the growth. There was always something mechanical that needed repairing; a water pump, hot water tank or the many fans that helped keep rooms cool. Equipment had to be oiled to prevent rust. This jungle bordered a desert but still had sufficient rainfall so the government figured crops could be grown.

The local men were friendly and tried to help, but things did not get off to a good start and they never got better.

The government had cleared a nice tract of land and left me one tractor to work the earth. It was a Ford with plow, disc, and harrow. There were also ditcher and cultivator tools that attached with a three-point hitch.

When I walked out onto the proposed site of the crop planting, I realized that the earth was very muddy, in fact too muddy. I was forced to wait three weeks for it to dry out enough to get the tractor in

I appointed Noe as foreman of the group of workers we had assembled. He seemed to command respect and was a little older than most of the men. We met every day and went over the operation of the tractor and the installation of each tool with the three-point hitch. The workers were all given turns driving the tractor and changing the tools. We had to use the main road around the village because the ground was wet. Discussions took place about what would be involved in planting and tending the crops. They were a happy, willing group, but had never driven anything prior so it was slow going. I spent extra time teaching Noe so he could help me instruct the others.

Finally, after about three weeks, things dried out and planting the crops became a viable task.

That first morning I sent for Noe and told him to get everyone together, that the site was ready. Instructions on driving the tractor in actual dirt were given the workers and then we let them go ahead and drive the tractor slowly while Noe and I walked along beside them. We eventually got the ten-acre site prepared and using stakes and twine, marked our first rows to be made with the ditching tool. I explained to them that the rows had to be far enough apart for the tractor to drive up and down and turn around. The tractor pulled a cultivating tool. This way, weeds would be removed and dirt would be restored in the rows where it had fallen out into the ditch between rows. If irrigation was necessary, we had rows for watering. We had a good water supply, as there was a big spring near the site.

Then we set about planting. We hand sowed corn, squash and tomatoes. We put in beans, both green beans and beans to be dried and shelled for later use. We devoted a large portion of the site to corn. We planted sweet corn in a third of that portion and the remaining two thirds in field corn. The village had been given a few oxen and cattle so the field corn would be used to feed the stock. Hay pellets were sent from the government also.

The government also provided a couple hundred chickens and ducks to the village. The locals ventured into the jungle and found wild banana and mango trees so they had a supply of fruit. Our venture into cultivating the jungle had begun.

Chapter 8

One of the things the government was trying to accomplish was to discourage the natives from eating the flesh of monkeys. It was a suspicion that this practice was making the people sick. Monkeys had been suspected at that time as carriers of the Ebola virus, which was dreaded around the world. The news broadcasts on the radio announced that Ebola originated in a jungle in the rain forest. Our surroundings were not that different although it was not considered a rain forest. The government campaign was more or less successful. At least the practice seemed to stop in our village.

The women cared for the chickens and ducks, feeding and watering them, gathering eggs and keeping their pens and coops clean. We kept a supply of Black Flag insect killer and used it often in the coops. This kept all bugs away.

The eggs were an excellent source of protein. There had been some banty chickens and roosters running loose in the village, but they hadn't been tended and their eggs hadn't been gathered so only a few of those found their way to a table.

When the crops were coming up nicely and the corn was about a foot and a half tall, a bad rainstorm hit, flooding the whole site. Everything washed out. We were all sick about it.

I got letters out to the government via a missionary who visited often. I inquired as to whether the weather patterns and rainfall in this area were unusual and reported our plight Two weeks later I received a letter from a specialist in the agriculture department who reported that they knew the weather may be marginal for growing these vegetables but was thought worth a try. If any of the vegetables could make it, even with occasional heavy rainfall, then the program was successful. Once again, I was told to let the site dry out and replant. New seeds were being sent

In the meantime, we busied ourselves with making roads, walkways and trails to the crop site, the school and our compound. Most of this work was done with picks, shovels and a couple wheelbarrows we were fortunate to have. The tractor and plow were usable for a little of the soft ground.

Again, the villagers were very willing workers. They sang as they worked and joked among themselves. Sometimes they pulled a practical joke on me, hiding my tools or jumping out from behind a tree, scaring me.

My foreman, Noe, had two sons 13 and 15 who were good workers and pleasant, dependable boys. The first time I wandered out a little ways into the jungle I got turned around and decided I better sit down where I was and not go any further. Fortunately, Noe's boys came after me. They said their father told them they better check on me. He knew I didn't know my way around. I yelled for help, but they hadn't heard my yelling until they were quite close to me. I didn't go out in the jungle alone after that, I always took the boys. The jungle is not an easy place to navigate. The trees and vegetation are so tall you can't see any landmarks. If you tried to make a permanent path, it would have to be trimmed every two days with a machete because the jungle grows right over so fast.

When the earth had dried enough to till, we began work again. Unfortunately, I had come down with a very high fever a couple nights before. I had never had anything like it. I could hardly walk and my skin looked a bit yellow.

The second morning of my illness, Marlena insisted, "I'll have John drive you to Campeche in the jeep. There is a good medical clinic there and you should go today. You know your medical and prescription costs will be reimbursed."

I answered, "Honey, I think you're right. I'll get ready." John was one of the other teachers and Marlena said she could combine his classes with hers that day. He pulled up within the hour and we set off for town.

Marlena had hastily put some cheese, crackers, hard salami and bottled water in a bag and said, "Don't forget to take this." We were glad to have the snacks and water, especially me with a fever. I was more thirsty than usual. We were able to take one of the government vehicles, a jeep, for our trip. The drive was very hard for me as I was so sick. We made it though and John was good company. He drove carefully and made sure I was alright, asking if I needed rest stops and encouraging me to sleep if I could. Sleep wasn't possible, but I was able to rest with my eyes closed.

When we got to the clinic, I was able to get right in to see a doctor. He seemed to know what was wrong. "Don't worry;" he said, "I think you have a fever from an insect bite. I've seen many cases just like this; the patient always has a yellow look to their skin. Oddly enough, the bite itself causes no itching or discomfort and is usually not visible by the time the fever breaks out. I'll send some medicine with you and you'll feel better in a few days."

We headed back and I felt relieved that I didn't have anything serious. We made it home and I thanked John and went immediately to bed after taking the first dose of medicine. In three days I was good as new.

We resumed our site preparation and everyone had turns on the tractor and equipment, then we planted the seeds as before.

This time, we almost made it. Our crops were only a couple weeks from maturity when again a bad rain came. The damage wasn't as great as before but still devastating. Most of our crops were ruined. A little stand of corn along one end of the site and some of the squash and beans made it, but not enough for a supplemental food source.

This time, I became very discouraged. We had worked hard and our work was wasted. I wrote the government official in charge of the program that perhaps we were attempting an impossible experiment. It was just a matter of time before the officials heading the program would come down for a routine check and find the problems themselves so I wanted to let them know first. I received a response to my letter indicating that it appeared that growing vegetables was not viable here and that the program would be dropped. My funding would cease after my contract ended at the end of the year, which was only three months away. After that I would receive no funds. I was concerned about sending support money for the care of my boy. And, of course, I needed to be able to help support Marlena.

Marlena's contract ended in three months as well, but she would have been able to renew hers without a problem. We started talking about what we should do. My choices were limited so I told her we might have to leave. I confessed to her that I had begun to feel confined so far from civilization. Our little apartment in the barracks and living conditions grew oppressive to me. I had only visited Johnnie twice and knew this wasn't enough, Marlena was getting tired of the living conditions in the village too and she knew I was unhappy there. We decided we must get out as soon as our contract ended

Even so, I knew I would greatly miss the jungle. I discovered the creatures to be fascinating and journeyed out with the boys whenever I had time. I loved seeing how the animals lived in their native habitat. The young alligators were so fast that when they grabbed a bird off the bank of the river, all you could see was a blur.

Large yellow or lime green pythons were undetectable for hours until they very slowly slithered along a tree trunk or branch. Monkeys chattered; leaping from tree to tree like the top of the jungle was their playground. Then there were the occasional jungle cats, graceful and cunning hunters.

We rarely saw the cats, but heard them growl quite close.

I developed a lifelong love and appreciation for exotic animals. I have kept iguanas, alligators, snakes and various birds of the jungle and creatures of the desert ever since then.

I ended up sending a wire to my father by way of a kind missionary who was visiting the village. I told Dad our location and asked him to please come and retrieve us as soon as possible. We had very little money and no vehicle. We had thought we could make it on the rather low wages indicated in our contracts because housing and medical expenses were furnished. Necessities including medicine, groceries, boots, shoes and mosquito netting had depleted our ready cash. The visit to the clinic in Campeche for my fever and the medicine I required took almost all of our remaining cash. Our contract stated reimbursement would be given us for medical expenditures, but unfortunately, it had not arrived. The government had promised to pay the balance of our wages at the end of our contract, but they usually took three weeks to actually get a check to us. We didn't want to wait any longer so wired headquarters asking them to send our checks in care of Marlena's parents.

Dad hadn't taken much responsibility in our household when I was growing up but he did care about me and did come to our rescue. It was a long tiring trip for him and I helped him drive on the way home and promised to send some money to him for gasoline for the car. We became acquainted again on this long car trip and bonded for life. He liked Marlena and she was charming and kind to him. In fact, after that, my father moved to wherever I lived. We didn't always agree on everything but respected each other's opinions.

Chapter 9

We hadn't been home for more than a month when Marlena found out she was pregnant. She wanted to be near her mother and sisters so we moved back to Mexico City. That was fine with me because I could spend lots of time with Johnnie and by now I missed the excitement of the city and my good friends there.

Marlena's parents let us stay with them until we got on our feet. I had not spent much time around Marlena's family before our marriage and upon our return it was good to get to know them. They were a happy family and made me feel I belonged.

I got a good job at a garage right away and started saving money. Things were looking brighter and everything went well.

I was relieved when Marlena had a normal pregnancy and a healthy boy. We named him Hugo. We were delighted. He was a cute round-faced fat baby with a funny way of looking at you. He talked in full sentences by the time he was a year old and was walking too. I said to Marlena,

"What a delightful child, he's happy and smiling most of the time."

She laughed and replied, "Yes, we are blessed to have him."

Marlena's father was a man with an easy smile, probably only 55. Alberto worked construction and was strong and muscular, of medium build. He was kind and soft spoken and doted on his family. He shared some of the cooking duties and was quite a good cook. I don't know if he thought much of me at first but over time, we became close and Hugo adored him.

Isabel, Alberto's wife, held Hugo close and cooed words of endearment to him, and then he would snuggle up to her and look up smiling, basking in all that attention.

Marlena had one sister, Ana, who was married and lived in Monterrey and a single brother just finishing a pharmacy course in Mexico City. This was a loving family with absence of misunderstandings and hard feelings, unlike my family when I was growing up. I vowed to contact my siblings and try to renew our relationship.

We started looking for a place to live and after about a month came across a nice home close to my job and Marlena's parents' home. It was roomy, had a nice little yard with a fence and a vegetable garden. I laughed when I thought about my bad luck with crops but we figured the vegetable garden would be great. We would eat healthy fresh vegetables and save some money.

We settled into the house, I planted my garden and Marlena fussed inside the house. She was a good homemaker. Again she made curtains, tablecloths and made our house a home. She was able to get a part time job at a store nearby and her mom watched Hugo while she worked. Our financial woes were gone and we were a lot happier.

I enjoyed being close to my boy Johnnie, too. I saw him often and brought him to our house for overnight visits. Marlena was loving and kind to him.

I resumed my art classes at the college in the evenings. I had missed my art work desperately. It was being creative once again and learning more about the craft I loved.

One evening, not long after I enrolled, three men in military uniforms came into the class and one tapped on my shoulder and picked one other student in the class as well. They then asked us to come with them. We didn't know what was going on

but they put us in a separate meeting
room with a few other male students they
had picked from other classrooms.

We were told that we were picked for
special Military Forces, for special duty in
the service of our country and that it
would be very prudent to agree to
cooperate immediately.

All of us were apparently chosen
because we were larger, more muscular
and fit than the other students. We were
all good students too. One other time we
noticed that military officers were looking
around but we had no idea they were
recruiting.

In Mexico, you don't tell the military
you don't want to serve.

Our instructions were to bring a few
belongings and be at the military base the
next day at 10 A.M. Marlena was worried
when I told her what I had to do and so
was I. We had no idea what was really in
store for us or how our lives would be
affected. The biggest concern was that we
would be apart. We were so happy and
couldn't even discuss being apart because
I choked up and Marlena cried; we
couldn't believe this was happening. I told
her that I could not refuse service after the
government recruited me, it just wasn't

done. We vowed to make this work and get through it. There was no way of knowing how long my stint with the government would last. I took Marlena in my arms and pledged my undying love to her. We both said true love like we shared would get us through anything and fell asleep in each other's arms. I left the next morning after telling them goodbye, embracing Marlena and giving Hugo a giant squeeze.

Chapter 10

We new recruits were taken to a
military base out of town, issued uniforms,
given the necessary inoculations and
housed in barracks under armed guard.
When I first looked at myself in the mirror
wearing my uniform, I realized I had
matured a lot in the last four years. I was
5'11" and weighed 160 lbs. My skin was
tanned and bronze and my hair and
moustache were jet black. Dark brown
piercing eyes were looking back at me. My
tall muscular frame made me a worthy
opponent and a favorite with the ladies. I
was very much in love with Marlena,
though.

Our training began immediately. We
were told that we would be Special Forces,
an elite group to do special assignments
for the government. Assurance was given
us that our families would be cared for.

Training began right away in hand-
to-hand combat, the use of all types of
weapons, self-defense maneuvers, survival
techniques, and martial arts. The trainers
explained to us that we may have to kill in
the course of duty.

Lying in my bunk at the barracks, I thought about that possibility. I was a peaceful man; more a lover than a fighter, I thought to myself. My stomach tightened every time I thought of taking another's life. Yet, from what we were being told, there was a distinct possibility that we could face this unfortunate situation. Our lives and the lives of our fellow soldiers would depend on the taking of another's life before they could take ours. A few of us talked about this scenario too and we were all uncomfortable and we even shared that we were actually scared and we were not bothered by sharing this confidence. There was nothing to be done though but go along with our training for now.

We were allowed phone privileges on our free time but there were only a couple of pay phones and a lot of guys wanting to use them. I was told that I could write to Marlena and my family; receive mail but to keep it at a minimum. We did write each other, all censored of course, but it was wonderful to get those letters. Ones from Marlena I most enjoyed. She wrote really sexy love letters, lamented about how much she missed me and of course I loved hearing that.

I kept in touch with my ex-wife Delores and son Johnnie by phone and letters. Delores received monies for Johnnie's care since I was on active duty.

Training took about seven months and we were tested stringently to make sure we learned everything sufficiently. The time went fast, we were shooting all types of weapons, blasting with big artillery, doing field survival.

We were kept busy all the time and the regimented activities and exercising succeeded in us reaching a level of fitness that none of us had ever experienced. We enjoyed it and had arm wrestling contests and tug of war bouts in the little off time we had. Tests were given us by specialists in each type of training we had received. Only about half of the recruits made it through this testing process.

Then finally, we were allowed a leave of three days and two nights to see our families. An announcement was made that if we didn't return on time, we would be picked up by the Military Police.

Marlena and I were so happy to see each other. We were crazy in love, renewed our feelings for each other and enjoyed the boys. Our friends put on a big dinner and I was able to see them all at one place. I couldn't discuss my military career so I avoided much mention of it and just told my buddies that I was still in training. Marlena packed a picnic another day and the boys loved that. My leave was over much too soon and I had to return to duty.

Chapter 11

Our first assignment was preparation for the site of the 1968 Olympics, which was to take place in Mexico City. We would be working with engineers from the Telavisa (television) station to install all of the electrical equipment for the games. Telavisa had two weeks of basic electrical training classes for us, divided us up in groups for our particular projects with their engineers and we then we went to work. They had the contract to install all of the televisions, electrical equipment, lighting, and sound equipment. The project was enormous and took over two months.

Still housed in the barracks during this work period, we were taken to work and back in military buses. We were given a two night leave and told not to discuss our work. Marlena and I took our son to the beach and enjoyed our time together. We relaxed and talked about plans for the future. Being apart was awful for both of us and I worried about Hugo, wishing I was there to help and care for him. We vowed again to get through the ordeal, to make the best of our time together and enjoy every precious minute that we had together.

When the job was completed at the Olympics, we were given a second leave of one week and again I was delighted to be with my family. Marlena was a kind mother and Hugo a delightful child. Her family was very supportive and lived close enough to be of help to her. They insisted on watching Hugo for a couple days while Marlena and I took off on a romantic getaway to a private resort in the foothills. The air was cooler, it was quiet and peaceful. We had a second honeymoon and the relaxation did us both good.

I also took time to write to my siblings but it was a bit awkward because I couldn't tell them much about my military obligation. I just told them I was in the supply department.

Chapter 12

Upon our return from leave, all of us in our special unit were called in for the next assignment. We were told we were going undercover as college students at the University in Mexico City. We were taught all about college life for a month.

They actually brought military officers, who had been teachers, in to give us the training we needed to move about a college campus unnoticed. College life suited me and I settled in easily, the classes were interesting. I had been a student so I knew what to expect. The social aspect was intriguing with many different kinds of people from many various walks of life. Many times during that period of time, I wished I had been privileged enough to attend a top university without money worries and take advantage of the many opportunities offered. I had a hard time understanding why students I met didn't appreciate their good fortune. They complained about school and studies, and it was all I could do not to berate them about their attitudes.

Ramon, one of the other undercover students, became a very good friend of mine. We were housed at the same apartment complex on campus. Ramon was handsome. He was in excellent physical condition, tall and muscular, with large hands and arms. His hair, jet black, was worn short and he wore no moustache. These features along with his large dark brown eyes and broad smile gave him a boyish look. Given his size, however, Ramon was definitely a man that could be disconcerting if he was angry about anything. He didn't talk a lot and when he did, he had thought about it beforehand. He was not at all spontaneous but intelligent and interesting. We enjoyed each other's company and got together often. Because of our undercover status we had to be careful not to be seen together too much. We usually enjoyed a beer or meal off campus.

Our objective, we were told, was to find out which students and/or student organizations were speaking against the government. Those contributing in any way to the political unrest by influencing other organizations off campus were to be reported as well.

Political unrest took place not only among the students, but they were getting an exceptional amount of backing from the working class and general population. The political views of the students were well received by many because they directly opposed those of the government.

There is no doubt that the students at the UNAM and IPN universities with their disturbances in the streets and their rowdy behavior in their schools, gave the police every reason to intervene. The demands of the students and protesters were ongoing through all the demonstrations. I was amazed at how innovative they were. The aeronautical engineering at UNAM came up with balloons that would automatically release propaganda upon reaching a certain altitude, showering thousands of leaflets on the people and sidewalks of Mexico City.

There were also many disturbances and violent incidents. One of the worst was when the soldiers attacked the Santo Tomas campus which was the bloodiest and most frightening incident till that time. The students took their wounded to the School of Medicine so they wouldn't be hauled off to jail. Because of this government retaliation in the midst of the student movement, women boiled water on their stoves and dumped it on the soldiers. They hunted soda bottles to fill with any flammable liquid to throw at the police. Molotov cocktails were the only real weapons the students and people had. If successful after tossed, one of these cocktails could blow up a vehicle and many found their mark. The students had zip guns, firecrackers and skyrockets. The fireworks didn't hurt anyone, but annoyed the military personnel because of the sound. People actually gathered stones, jars, cans and pieces of wood and paving blocks to throw if needed. They would take to the roofs to be able to throw things down if the military attacked.

The students were asking for a more democratic form of government. This was a huge civic awakening of an entire generation of young people. The students were drawing crowds of unheard of numbers at their protests.

The protest planned for August, 1968, was to be a silent one. To keep control of shouting and chanting at demonstrations, many young people agreed to tape each other's mouths shut, so their silent protest would be successful.

In fact, the demonstration in August at the Tlatelolco Square drew about a quarter of a million people. Many thought at the time that if the President had gone out on the balcony, confronted the crowd, he would have divided the demonstrators and won over a great number of them. The President's advisors did him no favors with their advice that day.

Several of us undercover students marched to avoid being noticed more by joining in and becoming a necessary part of the group.

The Government could not ignore the number of protestors and the diverse following of students. The administration felt compelled to take drastic measures. Protesters also included teachers, nurses, doctors, electrical workers, farmers and workers from many other professions Women were extremely active in this movement.

The protesters published this notice and following six-point plan in the El D'ia, newspaper on September 13, 1968.

"We have called this march to press for the immediate and complete satisfaction of our demands by the Executive Power. We repeat that our Movement has no connection with

the Twentieth Olympic Games to be held in our country or with the national holidays commemorating our Independence and that this Committee has no intention of interfering with them in any way. We insist, once again that all negotiations aimed at resolving this conflict must be public.

"The march will begin today, Friday the thirteenth, at four p.m. at the National Museum of Anthropology and History and will end with a public meeting in the Plaza de la Constitucion.

"The day has come when our silence will become more eloquent than our words, which yesterday were stilled by bayonets."

The students had developed this six-point plan:

1. Freedom for all political prisoners.
2. Revocation of article 145 of the Federal Penal Code
3. Disbandment of Corps of grenaderos.
4. Dismissal of police officials involved Luis Cueto, Rau'l Mendiolea, and A.Farias.
5. Payment of indemnities to the families of all those killed and injured since the beginning of the conflict.
6. Determination of the responsibility of individual government officials implicated in the bloodshed.

The Protest at Tlatelolco Plaza took place that fateful day, October 2nd, 1968, and the crowd numbered 600,000 people.

The government devised a plan that one of we undercover students would take a shot at a crowd control guard during this protest.

We were told that would enable the guards to start making arrests and break up the protest. We knew of no other plans by the army.

We had already marched in the previous demonstrations from the south to the center of the city, and in another from the north to the center of the city. Now in this third demonstration, our goal was: the Zocalo, one of the most imposing public squares in the world.

The protestors intended to take it over and protest beneath the balcony, the very balcony where the President of Mexico presents himself for public speaking on historic occasions. I knew there would be trouble as I figured the government would react unfavorably to such an enormous demonstration.

One of the things the protesters had felt strongly about was the destruction done when the army destroyed the Puerta de San Idelfonso, a stately four hundred year old building with hand carved wood everywhere and old terracotta tile floors. They could not forget that the army had occupied schools, and clubbed students, teachers and bystanders alike. The military had taken over several of the universities. The students had already prepared their demands and basis for the protest in the six-point plan. In my heart I secretly championed their cause.

We protesters marched behind a plain red flag the size of a billboard, held by poles on either side, each carried by a protester. Plain red flags were the customary choice for protests at that time. This demonstration took place at night. Bells were all ringing in the Cathedral and people poured out of hotels and houses and began applauding. The sound of the footsteps of hundreds of thousands of people was the only other memorable sound as we came nearer our destination. Thousands of hands were raised in the symbol that soon covered the entire city and that had been seen at public functions, on television, and at official ceremonies: the V ("We shall win") formed with two fingers. It was a spectacular sight when we entered the Square; all the lights had been turned on. There were bunches of flowers everywhere and many people carried lit candles and candles had been placed on the steps of most of the buildings. There were thousands of flickering lights in all. The huge plaza with the old buildings surrounding it was grand and the arched windows of the ancient cathedral majestic with huge stained glass windows. All of a sudden flares lit up the sky and what happened next was the frightful event known as the Tlatelolco Massacre.

As soon as the shooting started, two army helicopters came down dangerously low, circling right over the heads of the crowd in the Plaza and began firing on everybody. We could see the gray streaks of tracer bullets in the sky. Sharpshooters shot from the top of buildings into the street. Military forces fired round after round from machine guns mounted on their light tanks and armored transports. They shot at people in the protest march: students, teachers, anyone in their line of fire.

Chapter 13

Undercover students were not told that any of this was going to take place. As I mentioned earlier, we thought one of our group had orders to fire a blank bullet in the direction of the crowd control police and that the police would use that as an excuse to break up the protest. Our instructions were to wear white handkerchiefs wrapped around our right hands only at the demonstration so we wouldn't be arrested or manhandled by the police. There was no fear we would be noticed because there wasn't that many of us and we were not together in the street.

A shock was in store for us. When the shooting began no one seemed to care about us. We were shot at just like the rest of the crowd.

I was in the street, walking in the protest with the students when the gunfire broke out and I saw the slaughter and was momentarily paralyzed with fear at the killings I witnessed. It was inconceivable. Immediately my survival instincts took over and I ran out of the crowd, zigzagging to avoid gunfire. There were apartments up the street and I ran to one and banged on the door. No one answered and cold fear was gripping me as more bodies were falling.

People were screaming, running in panic and I banged one last time on the door and screamed, "Please help me, I will die" and just then an old woman answered the door. She opened it a tiny bit and quickly said, "Hurry, hurry." and opened the door a few inches and I burst in. She slammed the door shut and locked it.

Then she hurriedly led me upstairs into a small back bedroom and pointed to a tiny closet. "Get in there, I'll cover you." She threw a small coverlet off the end of the bed over me and said, "Do not come out, don't make a sound.

Then I heard her go downstairs as fast as she could. After about 15 minutes, I noticed the shooting had slowed noticeably. Then I heard the screaming of victims and yelling by police, and just an occasional shot fired. It seemed like forever, I could hear my heart beating and my own breathing. Twenty minutes later the old lady came up and got me out of the closet and we peeked out of the upstairs window. The scene we looked down on was that of death and destruction, with blood everywhere. The expression on her face was of horror. As I put my hand on her shoulder to try to comfort her, soothing words came to me but I couldn't even whisper them to her. I was unable to utter a sound.

We watched as the police came in right behind the initial horrible barrage of bullets and were clubbing and beating already bloodied people mercilessly. They arrested many protesters and threw them bodily into vehicles and took them to jail. Two thousand people were arrested. The army brought in trucks and speedily cleaned up the streets and hauled the bodies away. They washed much blood away by the morning's light using Army water trucks and fire engines with hoses hooked to the hydrants. In the pale dawn the immense square did not look like the murder site it had been the night before.

I waited with the old lady whose name was Carmen. She was short, with a slight figure and walked a little hunched over. Her salt and pepper hair was fastened up in a bun and the many lines in her face and on her hands showed her advanced age. Her eyes were small, black and deeply set in her small face. She wore a faded orange print housedress with a green cooking apron over it. She wore intricately carved silver earrings and bracelet. I made a mental note to bring a gift of nice jewelry to her.

I told her I would never forget her, that she had without any doubt saved my life and that I would be grateful always.

I commended her for her extremely quick thinking and actions over hot chocolate and a simple breakfast. She told me she was very glad she had let me in so that she didn't have to face the tragedy alone. Carmen said she had gone through tough times in her long life, had survived the death of two children and a husband. She did have a married daughter. Her husband was a businessman and they lived in Manzanillo. They had two children. It was still early that morning and we shared the feelings of horror and desperation about the scene we had witnessed. She told me not to leave until later that day because it would not be safe. Later, after writing my name, home address and phone number down for her, I insisted that she never hesitate to call on me for anything she may need or want. I gave her a hug and left the apartment.

Chapter 14

After the massacre I knew it would be necessary to report all to my military supervisor but I waited a couple days. I got in my car, which had been parked several blocks away because of the protest, and drove to a friend's home in the country. I had to regain my composure knowing that the military was at fault and what they were capable of.

There were no pictures in the newspapers of bodies lying in the Plaza because the Army troops would not allow it. The newspapers and magazines, radio and TV stations all reported that there had been an altercation. They reported that about 35 to 60 people were killed; some said nearly a hundred. There were no estimates higher than 150, when in fact the actual number of the dead was in excess of 375.

An awful situation immediately after the massacre was that families had loved ones missing and there were no death lists or names of prisoners posted anywhere. People were alarmed and grieving for their loved ones. They were furious too, but after this horrific event, they were frightened to make any trouble or annoy the government or troops.

Foreign news broadcasters were in the city to cover the Olympic Games, which were to take place a few days after the massacre. The foreign correspondents reported the carnage and began sending bulletins informing the entire world of what had happened.

Their reports of genocide and extreme violence endangered Mexico's prestige. A lot of the visitors from European countries began canceling their reservations, as did other visitors from around the world.

It was said that the killings at Kent State and Jackson State in 1970 paled in comparison to this tragedy. The terror and shock of this massacre has not been forgotten in Mexico.

Chapter 15

When I reported for duty a couple days after the massacre, I was called in with a handful of the remaining undercover members from the college. I saw my good friend Ramon come in and take his chair and was so happy he was alright and had gotten through the massacre unhurt. Orders to us were: put it behind us, things went wrong, absolutely do not talk about the event under any circumstances, and do not answer any questions or discuss the matter with anyone. We were given a two night leave.

My thought at the time was that we would all go our separate ways to our homes and be less likely to discuss the event among us. However, later that night Ramon and I got together for dinner in town and shared our experiences during the massacre and our fear of what may happen to us if we were to talk about any of it to the press or anyone. Ramon had been marching with the last protestors to enter the square. They heard the gun fire and ran for safety. He was shocked by the whole thing too and amazed when he heard my story. I went home to Marlena and Hugo after dinner and she was following the news of the massacre, but I did not dare mention anything to her. I just agreed with her what a terrible thing and we watched the news together. If she had known I was close to losing my life, it would have caused her so much worry. She would have been terribly frightened. Since I was not able to share my work particulars with her, she was spared the agony of knowing I was involved.

Ramon was the only person at this stage of my life that I felt I could trust. We enjoyed going out for a beer or a meal and I took Ramon home for dinners with Marlena and our boy Hugo often. We all had a great time playing cards visiting and laughing. Marlena liked Ramon too. Sometimes we went on picnics, other times car trips. Hugo loved playing ball with Ramon. These times helped us forget about our work.

On occasion, Ramon's parents invited us to their home for dinner and they made us feel welcome right away. Ramon's father, Ernesto was a retired college teacher. He was a tall, thin older man with an easy smile and in his retirement preferred to wear a worn western hat most of the time. He was a good cook and assisted Anna when they served big dinners. The pork or goat meat was cooked outside on the Bar B Q and it was always very good. His wife, Ana, was older also, probably 66 and she was short, round and jolly. She had a great sense of humor and really enjoyed people.

After dinner in the evening, Ernesto picked up an old guitar and invited us all out onto the porch where he played for hours and we all sang.

Chapter 16

Once back in service, Ramon and I settled in and were given other undercover assignments.

One was to investigate the CEO and managers of one of the large newspapers, find out about their true political loyalties and who their informers were. Things were being reported about the military decisions and actions and how badly certain criminals had been treated. Evidently our military bosses didn't like the way the reporting was done.

For the newspaper undercover job, we were provided completely furnished apartments. Socializing was necessary. We were posing as businessmen working for an advertising agency. Business cards were printed and we were issued temporary use of two ordinary cars. An office was rented; the sign on the door said "Gonzales Advertising Agency". A sign in the lower left window stated, "We have offices in five major cities in Mexico." There were agencies in other cities so this all checked out. Our bosses were thorough, intelligent men. They seemed to think of everything.

Fittings for business attire were arranged for us at a local men's clothing store. Our wardrobes consisted of business suits, shirts, ties and shoes. Ramon and I teased each other at how businesslike we looked. We enjoyed being dressed up and out of uniform for a change. We were encouraged to make friends with any of the staff we could, male or female and to listen for any useful information. The staff had a favorite bar where they were getting together after work. We became regulars. After several beers, these employees were talkative. After about four months of observation and research, we had found out the information we were to obtain and submitted our final report. Ramon, who was single, dated one of the editors of the newspaper and she confided in him some information that was extremely helpful. He hated to see this assignment end because he had to break up with her immediately and he had grown fond of her.

Sometimes we were assigned to cover elections. Suspicions and sometimes hard evidence of fraud have traditionally plagued elections in Mexico. There were even cases of voters with valid photo-ID cards being turned away because their names did not appear on voter lists. This raised concerns about the "shaving" of suspected opposition voters from the lists. We were stationed at the polling booths to observe everything. We were to watch that the ballots were counted properly and placed in sealed ballot boxes, which were then kept under military guard.

Our superiors informed us that Luis Echeverria, who was the Secretary of the Interior and had gained prominence for the 1968 Massacre, was running for El Presidente. He was the popular candidate of the party in power. There was a lot of coverage and speculation on TV and in the newspapers about the election.

When the election took place, Luis Echeverria won on December 1, 1970. My unit had been in charge of overseeing the election. Since he was the favorite with the party in power, we assumed he would be elected.

Chapter 17

Ramon and I discussed whether this change in power would make a difference in our jobs. We didn't think so, but we were mistaken. A week later, twelve of us in my unit were told to present ourselves in dress uniforms at the government mansion for a meeting with two Presidential advisors.

The meeting was short. We were called in, congratulated for our efforts and successes and given our next assignment. We twelve were to be El Presidente Luis Echeverria's personal bodyguards. This was a good promotion and recognition for our military service to date.

There were classes to educate us on the current political views of our new president, and his wishes about protocol, dress and chain of command. We were taught never to leave him out of our sight on our watch, and to check out every visitor to the mansion. At the same time, we were to be still, silent and undetected, so that we weren't spotted. Our new El Presidente didn't want to feel we were hovering. We could move through a crowd using special hand signals to communicate, and no one detected us. We were good at our job.

Luis Echeverria's new home, the Presidential mansion, was fitting for his position. It was an impressive three story older building. Large columns holding up the balcony came out over the massive, intricately carved front door. Entrance from the street was gained by passing through two large iron gates. Armed guards were posted at the gates and no one was allowed entry unless they were checked out and expected. The fence was heavy barbed wire with three feet of curling razor wire on top. The driveway, of large wide red brick, circled the big fenced courtyard to the front door of the mansion under the covered entryway and then curved back out a different gate. Armed guards were everywhere.

The front door opened into a large foyer with comfortable chairs. The formal dining room was grand with vivid murals of social and historic scenes of Mexico were painted on the walls. The dining table was huge with 22 chairs, ten on each side of the table and one at each end. A ballroom, the dining room and meeting rooms were on the first floor. The upper floors were for offices and living quarters with a wing on the third story for special guests. There was no yard, just a small protected courtyard in back.

The first big gala event after the election was a victory celebration. We bodyguards were spread out evenly and posted inside the ballroom for Mr. Echeveria's protection. Another unit did the outside surveillance. We were not able to eat, drink or do anything but keep our eyes on Luis and the room. We were relieved, when necessary, by a few extra officers.

The event was memorable and there were a lot of these functions. The food was prepared by the best chefs in the city and the bar supervised by professional bar keepers. The food and beverages were served by waiters in black suits with white shirts and black ties. The tables were set with many varieties of fruit, vegetables, cheeses and several big salads. Gracing the center of the table was a roast pig with an apple in its mouth. There were prime ribs of beef, whole roasted turkeys, and platters of oysters on the half shell as well as whole braised salmon on large ornate platters. The meat was served by chefs all in white uniforms with tall white hats. They wielded knives artfully and were obviously well trained. The dessert table was a vision with caramel flan, many varieties of pies, fruit glazed cakes and strawberries dipped in chocolate. A full sundae bar was included.

There were beautiful women of many nationalities, all nude, entertaining a party of males only. There were no family members invited. Cocaine was carried around and served on trays by the waiters. This came as rather a shock to us. It was hard for we young men not to stare at the women, some of the most beautiful in the world, but we did not, as we would have been immediately relieved of our positions.

Chapter 18

Unmarked black vehicles with dark glass windows had been issued to us as part of Luis' personal staff. They had no license plates. These cars could have easily been mistaken for Judicial Police cars. Ramon and I liked driving them. No one would bother us, as the judicial police are the most dangerous and feared force in the country. They do their work for the powerful government officials quickly and successfully without asking questions. No branch of the law seems to govern them. They also use rough methods to force detainees to sign confessions.

I always enjoyed working for Luis. The El Presidente liked my driving and often specifically asked me to drive him on outings or trips he took. There were often at least two other cars accompanying us, one in front and one in back. There were several times where we were followed and required to outrun enemy vehicles. Often our gunmen shot the tires and disabled the approaching vehicle. Sometimes we took a side road and whipped around and all drew weapons and when the vehicle in pursuit came upon us, we opened fire and kept Luis safe.

Shortly after one of these altercations when we had saved Luis' life, General Ortega and I were driving to town to get evidence on a case when I admired a pretty house we passed. He said, yes it is a nice home. I thought no more about it but a week later, the general came to my quarters, said he just needed a minute of my time. I jumped to attention and He got a set of keys out of his pocket, handed them to me and said, "The house you admired last week is yours. The occupants will be moved out by the end of the week and you can move your family in." I replied, "I don't know what to say, thank you so much. My wife will be so happy there." I couldn't believe it, the house was nicer than I ever believed I would own. Receiving the beautiful home was quite a surprise. This regime really knew how to show their appreciation and it reinforced our feeling that we were important and of course we felt good about continuing to serve. Others of my unit also were given completely furnished homes.

That weekend I had leave and went home, got Marlena and Hugo and showed them the house that would soon become our home. They were delighted and we were all so excited. Our new home was in a nice neighborhood with good schools close. There was a wonderful fenced back yard for the boys to play in.

We moved in a week later with help from friends and family. Some of our friends decided to throw a surprise house warming party for the following weekend. Everyone had a awesome time. Giving housewarming parties was a custom at the time.

As much as I missed Marlena, Hugo and Johnnie, I have to confess that my career was incredibly exciting and rewarding. I had learned so much and enjoyed the intrigue, the investigating and yes, even the danger was part of the excitement. My thought at the time was that the government would no doubt recruit and train a younger force and dismiss us one day. When that might happen, I had no idea.

Chapter 19

After two years, our unit of twelve was assigned to work under one of the Generals whose duty was national safety.

Often one of the rebel groups, there were several, would seize a town or hold someone hostage. Our task was to diffuse their activities swiftly. If there was a hostage, we would take several of their leaders into custody. That usually resulted in a freeing of the hostage.

Violence was unavoidable and part of the job. None of us liked it and we felt badly when it was necessary. We usually got together in order to discuss the unfortunate circumstances immediately after one of these situations. The aim was to avoid the same results in the future.

One of the toughest assignments we had was when a group of Zapata rebels seized several large towns in the southern state of Chiapas and began formulating demands. They have been active since Emeliano Zapata and followers began the quest to organize those eighty years ago. He and his followers championed their needs and garnered sympathy for the Indians in Chiapas as well as the migrant population of Mexico.

The Indians needed a champion.
They worked the whole year, suffering the
worst privations; lived almost naked and
were badly fed. The migrant population did
not fare much better.

The insurgents have always been
devoted to pursuing basic rights as well as
blocking environmental regulations and
tax breaks to the rich. They also sought
basic protection for workers.

Back in 1968, The Zapista rebels had
taken over large areas of territory and
made their own rules. These rebels were
tough. In 1869 their ancestors in
Xochiapulco, when they received word
they were going to be attacked, evacuated
the city and burned it to the ground and
they took to the hills. The Sixth Army
moved in and camped there. At two in the
morning, Xochiapulco soldiers descended
from their hiding places. They dragged
themselves laboriously on their stomachs
through thick fog, their machetes in their
teeth. Then they stealthily descended from
their hiding places evading the sentries in
the heavy fog. Pouncing on the sleeping
invaders they gave a savage howl. In a
letter written by a soldier to his friend he
related, "They pressured us severely."

Right before the Massacre of 1968, the rebels lent their support for the student movement. They asked the Government to meet with them for peace talks in their home state of Chiapas. Before these talks were scheduled, the massacre took place. The Mexican Army was immediately ordered to take back the territories.

Our group of Special Forces was sent in ahead of the army to pinpoint vital and strategic locations, mainly the rebel command post. We were to report what kind of firepower and ammunition the guerillas had and how many locations they were holding. These tough fighters were dispersing into the hills but were still a large presence and held the territories. They were counting on public sympathy, for justice of the Indians, and reforms of the political system.

After the Massacre, even these rebels knew the Government wasn't going to cooperate with them to the extent they had hoped and expected prior. Our orders were to stay in a small town near the territory they were holding because the local police and National Guard were still in power there. Dressed shabbily, we went into the territory and posed as farmers or miners wanting work. Sugar cane production was in full force at that time and there were silver and sulfur mining companies in the area as well.

After completing our investigation and filing our reports, we met at a small inexpensive restaurant that we liked. We were still in undercover garb; wearing old worn clothes and shoes, had grown scruffy facial hair, longer hair and most of us looked unkempt. Over a beer and dinner we discussed our week and shared our feelings that things had gone very well.

But that night we returned to our motel and the rebels must have learned of our government connections because they ambushed us at midnight. A handful of armed rebels tried to break in our door. Furniture and braces had been placed against the door every night in case of trouble. These fortunately made entry difficult.

Waking out of a sound sleep, we jumped into our pants and shoes while shouting at one another, "Grab your gun." "Put on your vest." "Call the others." "We need backup now!" "Call the Police!"

Our weapons were at our fingertips and we donned our new bulletproof vests immediately. We were housed in three separate rooms. I grabbed a phone and called one of the other rooms, and yelled, "We're being attacked. They're trying to break down our door. Tell the others." The officer replied, "We're on our way." We heard the noise, alerted the others and called the police." They immediately ran to our aid, weapons ready. One of the guerillas posted down the hall saw the first officer approach and took a shot at him. The bullet didn't penetrate his vest and the officer returned fire, killing the guerilla. The fear was that the rebels would come at us in numbers and we weren't sure if the police would be there in time to take the pressure off.

In the meantime the guerillas tried to shoot the locks off our door and we hollered "Halt and cease fire." They didn't, so we shot right through the door in between the reinforcements and wounded three of them. They fell outside and others of their group came toward us from behind cover across the parking lot. We could look out the window but had to do it fast. They shot at the window a couple times. We shouted again, "Cease fire and drop your weapons or we'll kill you now."

They stopped and dropped their weapons, and I yelled, "Come and get your wounded and get out of here." Another of our officers yelled, "All of you vamoose or die here". The rebels knew they were done and left.

The police arrived about five minutes later; made sure we were all right and assisted in a sweep of the area to make sure none of the enemy was hidden. Watches were set up to make sure none returned.

It all happened so fast and ended just as fast, but we knew it was a very close call. The army moved in the next day and drove the guerillas back from territories they held.

Chapter 20

There were the instances of drug traffickers we were told to apprehend and arrest. Drug enforcement specialists came to the base and gave intense special training to us before we went on assignment. This was always dangerous work, as drug traffickers were usually armed and their plans well thought out. They had back up plans as well. The Drug Enforcement Department needed extra help whenever we could assist because drug trafficking was prevalent.

On undercover jobs, while tracking assassins or criminals we often gained valuable information about trafficking or undercover illegal operations.

We were taught how drug traffickers usually operated and where. Information was given us naming the known drug lords working in Southern Mexico at that time. The many methods of operations were discussed at length. Specific inst-ructions were given us regarding our handling and turning over of confiscated drugs, money, vehicles, and seized property to the Drug Enforcement Dept. Calling for backup officers before trying a drug raid was of paramount importance because of the danger. We were tested and worked with teams of experienced Drug Enforcement Specialists before we were given assignments on our own. This training lasted three months.

Most of the busts and arrests were fairly run of the mill; you've seen them on television or at the movies. A few, however, were memorable.

One such case began when the DED called us after receiving a tip from an informant that a sizable delivery and sale were to take place soon. The buyer was a well known and dangerous drug lord, Ernesto Commancho. He had been operating between Mexico City and L.A. Fortunately; we had undercover officers investigating the same people because of information elicited from the driver of a car after a routine traffic stop. The driver was in possession of a felony amount of cannabis. He was arrested, interrogated and finally told the officers his source for the pot and the names of the dealers. We recognized the names because we had been on the case for months. Undercover officers were infiltrating the sellers' operation and the buyers' as well.

Concerned because it appeared to be a sizeable bust we staffed the operation well. There was a lot to be done. We needed to know how many people were involved. What type of weapons might they utilize? Cameras, tracking devices and recording equipment had to be installed. The neighborhood where the bust was to take place had to be protected. When the time came and we knew where the site would be, officers would stage a phony emergency and close the major streets nearby

We were making plans rapidly; we did not know the place of the buy or the place where the buyer would take a load this size for distribution later.

We formed five teams, each with two agents and one sharpshooter. One team installed surveillance equipment and monitored it. Ramon's team was to infiltrate the gang. They were to hire on as workers. These two teams were successful and reported to my team. We remained ready and waiting for information from the others and made our plans accordingly.

The remaining two teams worked out the phony emergency plan and obtained five unmarked cars of different models and colors for us. They oversaw the installation of the best radio equipment in each car and worked out codes and signals for us to use. We all kept in close contact.

Finally, one of our agents, listening on a recording device, heard the boss Commancho say the location of his proposed purchase. Commancho was clever and none of his underlings knew when or where the sale was to take place. Only he and his right hand man, Levi, knew.

The purchase by Commancho from the unknown buyer was to take place at a commercial garage on skid row. We still didn't know when, however.

Fortunately, a few days later, Ramon overheard the date of the transaction. It was to happen in two days.

When the day came we were all in place and ready. Word came over our radios that a white bakery truck and a black Tahoe had pulled up to the garage. The team working with the gang had orders to place electronic tracking devices immediately on any vehicles that arrived at the garage.

Two men with briefcases got out of the car and headed for the office in the building. One was Commancho, a Mexican of medium build with black hair and no moustache. He did have a noticeable scar on his left cheek. We had studied photos of him. The other was Levi, obviously his bodyguard.

They were both dressed in business suits. Commancho moved stealthily his eyes darting seeing everything. The two looked too slick to be businessmen. Commancho was all in black, both suit and shirt and Levi in dark brown. They were armed; we could tell they had shoulder holsters.

The driver of the bakery truck was a huge man with long dark hair pulled back in a pony tail. He wore dark glasses and work clothes and boots. He looked mean with a constant sneer on his face. In the cab with him was another man, also in work clothes. He was smaller, his hair longish. He seemed nervous, jumped out of the cab, looking around the whole area checking it out. The garage door opened, the driver swung the bakery truck around and backed into the big bay. The contents inside were then loaded into the truck. The driver never got out of the truck. His passenger acted as a lookout. The driver had a sawed off shotgun sitting right next to him and the lookout, believe it or not, had a western pistol sticking out of a coat pocket and kept his hand on it the whole time. After the truck was loaded, it sped off with Commancho and Levi followed in the Tahoe.

Ramon said later that the two men had gone in the office and handed two briefcases containing large amounts of cash to a man. The man inspected the cash, and then walked out.

As soon as the loading was completed, the Tahoe and truck sped off. One team arrested the man in the garage; his name was Arturo and had no rap sheet or reputation to date. We couldn't figure how he got mixed up with the likes of Commancho on a deal this size. He appeared to be an unknown.

The confiscated briefcases contained the equivalent of $250,000. The property and contents were also confiscated.

Our team followed the bakery truck and Tahoe. Tracking devices had been placed successfully on them, so we were able to follow without being seen. We left the busy part of town. About seven miles out of the City, they turned into an upscale neighborhood and pulled up to a large home. It was an ordinary home, attractive, painted white with red trim and had a landscaped yard. All our teams were in place. Each team had a sharpshooter and we all wore bullet proof vests.

The emergency was staged with no sirens, just officers in uniform placing signs saying, "Road closed because of broken water main." We stopped a couple blocks away and hastened on foot to the house.

They were unloading the last of the load. The truck driver jumped back in the cab, and his sidekick was closing the back door on the truck. One team was hiding inside the house and apprehended Commancho and Levi quietly as we rushed the three outside. The driver, his lookout and another worker were all arrested swiftly without incident. The element of surprise was our big 'ace in the hole'. Fortunately everything went smoothly and we were relieved it was over. Commancho had been fighting mad when he was arrested but knew he had no chance. The bad guys were gagged, wrists and ankles cuffed and taken to jail.

The big truck driver had started yelling threats for about a minute before he too was gagged and cuffed.

This turned out to be a huge bust. My team and one other remained at the house. We confiscated 550 pounds of pot,

150 pounds of cocaine, scales, packaging equipment and some sacks of crystal meth. The drug house would become government property. A new corvette that was in the garage and the Tahoe were confiscated as well as the delivery truck. There were also shotguns, pistols and accounting ledgers. The ledgers contained valuable information regarding bank deposits resulting from drug sales and entries pertaining to other drug transactions. There were also two safety deposit box keys. No doubt we would find cash in those. The investigation didn't end with that bust and police made more arrests in connection with this operation. We were commended for our efforts.

Chapter 21

Mexican political history has shown that the country has never experienced a peaceful transition of power between opposing political forces. For this reason, we always had investigations of official corruption assigned to us. A file of unsolved assassinations was investigated on an ongoing basis. There were also a number of cases being investigated of those suspected of having conspired to assassinate a government figure. These assignments were all dangerous because the perpetrators would kill rather than be exposed.

We were called on routinely to act as bodyguards for Luis and his people. Sometimes we guarded visiting dignitaries, sometimes generals from out of town. We did our jobs well, but again, sometimes weapons were used and there were deaths. We took no pleasure in having to kill anyone. The incidents were very hard for us to get over and our consciences suffered these deeds even though all was done in the service of our country.

To tell you how things were in Mexico, I will relate an adventure or two. There were many assassinations of political figures posturing to gain power or win elections. Luis knew that he was in a certain amount of danger at all times.

One morning, Luis called me to his office and said he wanted me to drive him to Mexicali. The usual two teams of guards were to accompany us. These teams would each be in separate vehicles. El Presidente had routine meetings at a government building in town. He figured the trip would be three or four days.

We stayed at a government house when we were in Mexicali; it was one reserved for Luis whenever he needed it. It was a spacious adobe home, fully staffed, with a valet, cook and two servants. Comfortable leather couches and easy chairs were in the sitting room. There were coffee and end tables made of the finest hardwood with designs carved by expert

Mexican craftsmen.

Our sleeping quarters were large, with easy chairs, footstools and lamps, and full bathrooms. The beds had fine mattresses, soft down pillows and the comforters were thick, hand quilted, in bright turquoise and yellow. Marlena would have loved this room.

The grounds were fenced and had a white metal carved gate about 8 feet tall and 15 feet wide. A guard stood on duty at the entrance.

After Luis had completed his meeting the second day, he instructed me that just after dark, I was to drive him to a secret meeting at a home located up on a mountain pass, out of Mexicali. The rest of the team was to accompany us. Luis said that no one knew of this location and that he hoped there would be no trouble.

Two armed guards were in the car with us, one in front with me and one in back with Luis. One car in front of us held three armed guards and a driver, as did the car behind us. We headed up the mountain pass. The road was narrow and treacherous with many curves, and sheer cliffs. We had been traveling about 20 miles when we came around a curve and, out of nowhere, a big dark colored car raced up behind the guard car right behind us. They fired a couple shots at the guard car, but our officers saw the lights fast approaching behind them and weapons ready, returned fire immediately. Our officers had long-range rifles and other weapons just in case they needed them.

We had to keep moving. I drove as fast as I possibly could to try to outrun the assailants. It was a dark night and the road had no reflectors, and no guardrails. The lead car stayed well ahead of us. The bullets didn't slow me down.

Up the mountain we raced going sometimes on two wheels around curves. Sometimes the shooting let up as we'd round a curve ahead of our assailants. Then we could only see reflections of their lights. When they caught up to our car behind, another exchange of gunfire took place. I barely let up on the gas, just drove as fast as I could. Fortunately our team in back soon shot the driver of the assailants' car and it went right off a cliff. We saw the fire when their car crashed below. It hadn't taken our officers long to disable the enemy, but the moving vehicles made it difficult. I suddenly realized that I was sweating profusely. There was no stopping now until we reached our destination.

After the car went over the cliff, we saw no other lights. We got on our radios and shared concerns that there may be more trouble up ahead so the lead car was vital at that time.

We slowed down and proceeded up the mountain. Fortunately, no more trouble awaited us and we delivered Luis to his meeting. He thanked us for our handling of the situation. Late that night, we made an uneventful return to the Government house in Mexicali.

Upon investigation, we found out that the gunmen were hired killers working alone. Obviously they had been hired to kill Luis by a political enemy. Our investigative trail came to a dead end after we actually found out who the assassins were. We were unable to get any evidence on the actual person who hired them. The person or persons who hired the job done were obviously accomplished and clever, as we could not pick up a trail at all. The car had been rented by the assassins with no other connections. No bank transfers or transactions had taken place in the many accounts we checked on. The assassins would have probably been paid in cash if the job was successfully completed. The case remained open as long as Luis was El Presidente. Later, it was no doubt closed for lack of evidence.

Chapter 22

Another high-speed chase took place another time when we were accompanying Luis by car from Rumorosa to Tijuana. We had received word that we may have trouble because it was in the newspaper that El Presidente was making visits to various towns. The enemy should have figured that if we knew the trip was public knowledge, we would certainly have extra security in place. Instructions were given us regarding every detail of our travel. Extra security was put in place for this entire trip. Armed guards were posted to watch our vehicles, to make sure they weren't tampered with. More guards were assigned to secure the hotel we stayed in. Local city police escorts were supplied us in town and as we left. A fully armored, bulletproof car was issued us for the trip and we were advised that there would be roadblocks with security checks at either end of the pass. Again, it was a high pass with lots of curves. Our usual cars with the same drivers and armed guards traveled in front and behind of us.

We left Rubarosa and the city police escorts accompanied us out of town but we hadn't reached the first security check.

All of a sudden, our lookout in the car behind us said over the radio, "There are two cars behind us gaining at a very fast rate of speed. The roadblock is a short distance ahead. Take off and get to that. We'll do some interference with smoke bombs and gunfire if necessary. You should easily make it to the roadblock with no problem." The officer in our car answered, "We copy, I'm calling ahead to the road block, and they may be able to send help from there."

"Roger," our lookout answered, "We'll catch up with you there."

Our motorcade made it easily to the road block though we were traveling very fast. The lead car and I were both averaging about 90 mph. It was about 17 miles until we reached the roadblock. I was experienced at this type of driving, but it was a big responsibility to keep Luis safe. The smoke bombs had worked; the cars trying to apprehend us were unable to see and had to stop. The officers at the roadblock had immediately dispatched two police cars to aid us and they whipped past us, and then skidded around behind us just after we had tossed the last smoke bombs out ahead of the enemy.

There were no further incidents on

that trip. After all the excitement, we were relieved to settle down and relax a little bit.

The guys and I talked about the incident over beers the next evening. It was a short chase but could have gone bad if things hadn't worked out the way they did. We shared our perspectives about the events and visited about safety precautions. Opinions were shared as we were always trying to improve on our plans. If we devised anything that would work, we implemented it right away.

Once again Luis thanked us for our quick thinking and for delivering him safely to Tijuana. He was an appreciative man. Some of the military personnel didn't care for him. They thought he was arrogant and a bit rude. I did not. He was a proud man and had worked hard to achieve his present political status. He was all business and didn't have much of a sense of humor, but he was interesting to talk to.

Luis was intelligent and had theories and reasons for his particular political views. If we asked about current politics or certain articles in the newspaper placed by the opposing party, he was glad to explain all the particulars to us from his point of view.

I was still given regular leaves and Marlena was accepting of my situation even though she would rather I wasn't in the military. The home that was given us was most enjoyable and the yard perfect for the boys to play in. Marlena brought Johnnie home to play with Hugo and many times made sure the visits coincided with my leaves so I could enjoy the boys.

My bride and I were still crazy in love. I phoned often and talked to Marlena at length, wrote love letters and when with her, tried to show her how much I loved her. She assured me that she was managing alright but would be overjoyed if I was relieved of my duties and came home for good. Time went on and there was no way for me to know the duration of my military service. Feelings of apprehension plagued me then because I was away from home so much. Still, even though I missed Marlena and the boys desperately I have to be honest, the incredible excitement and challenges of my work suited me. It was a time that my physical strength and mental prowess were both excellent and I felt I contributed my all to the service of my country.

I will tell you of a strange situation

that occurred during our term of service. A General had come from his post in Monterrey to the mansion in Mexico City for a meeting with El Presidente. After the meeting; we were told that while the General was in town, he was to be shown a good time. Ramon and I were told to procure a female escort for him. If he wished to enjoy any of the local entertainment or nightlife, we were to drive him, and act as bodyguards while he was in town.

Of course we were discreet and stayed at a distance. We were used to being almost invisible in our line of work.

The General was a distinguished middle age man, quite nice looking, stood tall in his uniform and had an air of authority about him. We were introduced to him and then visited with him about what he'd like to do while in Mexico City. He expressed his wish to go out on the town to a nightclub or two to enjoy a few drinks, music and dancing. Arrangements were made for a young woman to escort him. Rebecca was one of the elite call girls who were familiar with high-ranking government officials. She knew how to conduct herself, curtail drinking and keep her mouth shut. She knew not to give out any of the information overheard in conversations while she was an escort. After we picked her up at the arranged time, we took her to meet the general at the lounge in his hotel.

She was stunning, about 25, blonde, perhaps of Scandinavian descent. Her hair was pinned up on top of her head with tendrils trailing down the sides of her face and the back of her neck. She was quite sexy. Her dress was of red silk, low cut but not too revealing. A black loosely knit wrap graced her shoulders. Black high heels adorned her feet and showed off her legs. She was tall but not as tall as our visiting General.

She was very professional and when introduced to the General, smiled, took his hand, and told him how pleased she was to meet him. He was obviously pleased to meet her. He asked us to take them to a couple nice nightclubs so we headed up town. They had drinks and danced at the first club and we stayed discreetly back away from them but still keeping watch. The General was having a good time and asked us to take them to another club where they danced a bit more then ordered a light supper and after dinner drinks.

At about two A.M., he asked that we

take them back to his hotel. We were
relieved of our duties by a new team of
bodyguards. They would remain in the
hotel on watch until shift change the next
day.

About four o'clock in the morning our
phone rang and it was one of the
bodyguards on duty; he told me an awful
thing had happened. Rebecca had come
screaming into the lobby with only a thin
negligee on and told the bodyguards that
the general must have had a heart attack,
he wasn't breathing. An ambulance had
been called immediately. I called Ramon
and we dressed hurriedly and went racing
to the hotel. Rebecca confided to us that
during sex, the General all of a sudden
gasped, and then lost consciousness, half
falling on top of her. He must have had a
major heart attack because by the time
our team reached the room, just a few
minutes later, he was dead. To protect the
General's reputation, they got Rebecca out
of the room, told the ambulance drivers
when they arrived minutes later, that he
had been alone. The ambulance drivers
took the General to the hospital. He was
pronounced dead on arrival of cardiac
arrest.

Later that day Ramon, the two guys

on the other team, and I talked about the General's misfortune. Of course it was a tragedy but, as expected, someone said, "Well if it's your time to go, it sure is the best way to go."

Then someone else said, "Think about this when you are in bed with your woman next time."

I said, "I know I will."

Even Luis chided us the next morning. With a stern look on his face, he strolled over as we were getting ready to go on duty at our different posts and said: "Gentlemen, I thought I told you to make sure the General came to no harm while he was under your care. I thought you were all excellent body guards?" We just looked at him not knowing how to respond. After a moment, he grinned and said, "No one can protect a guy in that situation, you must have gotten him a really good escort."

"We did sir," I answered.

Luis chuckled, then said, "Carry on men."

"Yes Sir," we answered in unison and went about our day.

Ramon and I were usually on the same assignments. I trusted him to watch my back and he felt the same about me.

All members of our unit were top notch; we all worked as a team. There were rough times with stakeouts and arrests. Danger and life threatening situations were part of our everyday lives. It sounds unfeeling, but we had to accept the violence and suppress our emotions.

In one instance, Ramon and I carried one of our guys bodily out of an apartment complex after a drug trafficker shot him. He lived but was in the hospital for a couple weeks and he wouldn't have made it if we had not gotten him immediately to the hospital.

Chapter 23

A letter arrived from Carmen, who saved my life at the massacre. We corresponded regularly. On my next leave I took time to visit her and take the gift of jewelry I had found for her. A week earlier, I had been in town and stopped at a jewelry store to see if they had anything I liked. There in the case was a perfect large turquoise pendant set in silver inlaid with a smaller piece of coral and a bit of black ebony. A pin fastener was attached to the back of the pendant so it could be worn alone as a brooch. The matching bracelet and earrings were stunning, too, and I purchased the set and had the jeweler engrave: "To Carmen with gratitude, I will never forget you, Manuel" on the back of the pendant. The jeweler said, "Must be for a special lady, huh?"

"Yes, she saved my life, Amigo," I answered.

He said, "She really is special." The jeweler wrapped the items nicely in three separate gold boxes, and then wrapped all the boxes together in bright red and orange paper with bows of deep blue ribbon. The artist in me thought, "What great colors for Carmen."

I called Carmen, and she said the next day was convenient for a visit. I told her I'd be there before noon. She said "Oh, you must have lunch with me, I seldom have a guest."

"Wonderful, I'll look forward to it," I answered.

Carmen greeted me wearing a bright red print dress with a yellow apron over it. She reached up and gave me a loving hug and kiss on the cheek. I lifted her off the ground and swung her around. When I put her down, she giggled and said, "Oh Manuel, it's so nice to see you, come on in. We'll visit and have lunch."

I said, "Yes, we've got some catching up to do."

The table was set with a bright green plaid cloth and yellow dishes. On the table were a variety of fruits, ham and salami, and some soft Mexican white cheese. She had made tortillas and they were warm and good. Dessert was a caramel flan. We shared conversation and talked about the political items that had been in the news most recently. After dessert she said, "Is there any chance you could drive me to town, I've got two birthday gifts to buy and a few groceries. It would save me taking the bus."

"Well of course, whenever you are ready. I'll help you with the kitchen, but first I have something for you."

I went to my car and got the package out of the glove box and brought it back in and handed it to her. "This is for you."

"Oh you dear, Manuel, you shouldn't have." When she opened the first box containing the pendant and read the engraving, tears came to her eyes, "Thank you so much. Oh, the pendant can be used for a pin also, and I love the bracelet and earrings. I'll treasure these and wear them often."

"You're so welcome Carmen. Now let's go to town."

We got her shopping done, sipped a soda in a shady courtyard and I took her home just before dark.

"Thanks so much," she said, "Now write when you can."

"I will," I said, "Goodnight."

Chapter 24

Short regular leaves were allowed. Being away was increasingly difficult. My time at home was important to me. These visits were all that kept me going because they afforded me some badly needed relaxation. Our assignments had been many and stressful. I felt more tired than I ever had before. The gruesome schedule was wearing me down.

My wife was pleased because the checks arrived regularly from the government and she had a job she enjoyed. Her mother and sisters loved our son, Hugo, and helped her with his care. Marlena missed me all the time, though, and told me so often. I was concerned about her happiness.

I didn't want to worry Marlena too much before the elections but when she asked me if there was a chance my career may come to an end, I told her it was likely. I told her not to worry, that I had a lot of experience and would be able to get a good job. As I reassured Marlena, I was secretly worried.

During my military career, I had no financial worries. Even though I was weary and worn out, my work had been exciting and gratifying. Being away from my family was hard though and I yearned for a more normal life.

Ramon and I talked about what we would do after the elections and discussed possibilities and ideas. We talked of a fishing trip or a few days at the beach.

Chapter 25

As the time for elections approached, it was obvious that the president"s political party backed a new candidate, Jose Lopez Portillo and worked hard to promote him.

Luis had suffered much unfavorable public opinion because of the way he had handled issues while he held office. His was one of the most negative reputations of any Mexican President. He was accused of irresponsible government spending, increasing inflation, and cronyism, which was obvious because he appointed his good friend and eventual successor, Jose Lopez Portillo, Finance Minister. During Echeverria's term there were violent devaluations of the peso as well as rising debt. The country's external debt soared and this caused the ruling party, in terms of its economic policies, to gradually lose prestige at home and abroad.

Extensive television and newspaper advertisements were done by the party (PRI) to bolster the popularity of Jose Lopez Portillo. Larger than life size pictures of the new candidate were placed on billboards in many strategic locations.

Extensive radio advertisements were heard often and flyers were distributed.

When the elections took place, sure enough, Jose Lopez Portillo was elected and a new regime placed in power.

Chapter 26

I was discharged from my military service. The new president had his own people for all major positions.

The timing was great for me as I yearned for a normal life. My exciting, yet demanding, military career was over. I had mixed feelings but really felt it was a great experience and I served my country well.

We still had the lovely home that was given me. I promised Marlena that the first thing I was going to do was take her away on a special trip, our second honeymoon. Her mom would watch Hugo and then, I told her, "We'll take a nice trip with the boys before I take a job." I received mustering out pay and we had savings so it was a perfect time to kick back and enjoy life a little. Marlena had a vacation coming so we were all set. I figured to look for a job after spending some long awaited quality time with my family.

Ramon and I got together often and talked about how different our lives would be now that we weren't in the military. We had made some plans too. I had promised to take Ramon to the Campeche Jungle. He and his father wanted to take me to a bass lake where they had enjoyed fishing for years.

He told me he thought he was ready to settle down and hoped he would meet the right woman. I told him that living a normal life now, he would no doubt meet someone soon and be able to court her properly and marry. Of course, we spent a lot of time visiting about many of our past adventures.

We still were under orders not to divulge anything about our activities while in the service, so we could only talk to each other about them. Sometimes our whole unit got together and talked privately about old times. We vowed we would not lose track of each other, that we would always remain friends. Incredible experiences that we had all shared bonded us in a special way.

Marlena and I drove to the beach and stayed at quiet, romantic resort. We spent lots of time talking about our future and, of course, spent hours in each other's arms. Our quiet dinners in the evenings on the veranda, overlooking the ocean, were perfect.

A couple weeks later, we packed up the boys and took them to the mountains where it was cooler and they ran and played. Little boys always collect a variety of sticks and rocks and pine cones, things of nature, then bring them home. These treasures fulfilled their instinct to bring home things from the wild. Camp fires were enjoyed late in the evenings after hikes during the day. We all had a great time and after returning home I set about finding work.

Chapter 27

Luis knew I was looking for work and recommended me for a good paying job with a prominent, well-to-do owner of a large construction company.

Gustavo Sanchez hired me as a bodyguard and driver for him and his family, because kidnapping happened occasionally.

He was a tall man about 55 with black wavy hair and slim build. He was the recipient of many government contracts while Echeverria was in power and evidently had a good reputation and didn't get involved in politics because as soon as the new presidente was in office, he was still given contracts.

Gustavo was the kind of man that looked you right in the eye and had a ready smile. When he shook my hand I sensed that he liked me. He and his family lived out of Mexico City about 120 miles on a big estate. He had a wife, Perla, and two daughters, Tia and Ida. Perla was probably fifteen years younger than her husband.

On my first day reporting to work, Gustavo brought his wife out to meet me. Perla walked out of the house with stunning black hair that fell to her shoulders. She was blessed with a fairly light complexion and large dark brown eyes framed by long black lashes. Her figure was perfect. When I looked into her eyes, I knew right then we had some kind of connection and I thought," Oh hell, I've been in this spot before."

Gustavo was wealthy and bandits were prevalent. I was to drive a special van, built for them, which was large and rugged, able to go over any terrain they wished and bullet proof.

The estate included ranchland, horses, and cattle with a very spacious adobe home and outbuildings all painted terracotta. The buildings sprawled atop a knoll and the spectacular view was unobstructed. From the front of the home you could look down into the flatland where there was a banana plantation, boasting many shades of green.

The kitchen was large with Mexican tile in bright colors on the countertops and drain boards. The kitchen floor had oversized brown tile, each measuring about 20x20 inches. Light streamed in from a south window, enough to be nice and light but not enough to make the room too warm. A big vase of fresh flowers was always on the massive table and the cook usually had fresh baked cakes and cookies set out in containers in the kitchen.

The atmosphere was inviting and I felt comfortable strolling into the kitchen anytime for a cool bottle of soda or a cup of coffee and some cookies. I never missed a chance to tease the cook, Emily, a sweet, kind, heavyset woman, and she teased me right back. The dishes she prepared were among the finest I have ever had the pleasure of enjoying. She did the entire cooking for the family and the only time she called for extra help was if Perla and Gustavo were entertaining. Then she hired a lady in the community to assist her.

A large atrium was in the center of the house with a walkway straight through the back to the courtyard. Cobblestone bricks set in paths around the garden assured unobstructed viewing of the plantings of bougainvillea, different varieties of cacti, poppies, and a poinsettia hedge. In these gardens, roses also bloomed because the lady of the house loved them. When you walked out into the courtyard the fragrance of the many roses was always pleasant.

Down the slope from the front of the home, twenty acres were planted in field corn for the stock. Nearer the home, a two acre garden was tended by the gardener, Cisco. Sunflowers were planted on two sides of the garden. There was sweet corn, vegetables and many varieties of peppers. In between the wide corn rows, varieties of squash were planted. In the fall the corn field was colorful with the many kinds and sizes of squash.

Cisco kept his fine garden and was allowed to take to market whatever produce the family didn't use. He was able to make some extra money and appreciated that. Cisco was a stocky man with a quick genuine smile and great sense of humor, a real happy go lucky fellow. He loved gardening and caring for the farm animals. He was soon my good friend. There were ranch hands and workers on the ranch, but Cisco was the only one that I made friends with. Keeping in touch with him and his lovely wife, Lupe was important to me for years after my work there on the ranch.

The whole estate was designed so that they were self- sufficient, growing as much of their own vegetables, meat and poultry as they could.

In the fields as you looked down from the house, next to the crops of bananas and vegetables, a herd of about 100 long-horned Mexican cattle grazed.

Looking at the expansive views always sparked the artist in me. I decided to bring a sketch pad and a few canvases to try and capture a scene or two. It was good to be an artist again. When I was in the military, there just wasn't time for that sort of thing.

The fence posts on the ranch were made of heavy rocks around large posts set into the ground. Ocotillo branches with the thorns still on were used for the fencing material. These long branches like cactus dry and then are quite strong. The fences kept the cattle in and the bandits out.

There were also a dozen horses, the finest money could buy and the family rode often. Trails wound all across their property and deep into the foothills. I accompanied the family on most outings. A very well-trained horse was assigned to me by Gustavo. My mount was trained to stay still if guns were fired and if left with the reins on the ground, to remain in that spot till the rider returned. He didn't have to be tied.

Running through the ranch was a creek, the source of water for the crops and stock. The family would occasionally fish and go down and swim in the creek. It was cool and they all liked to play in the water.

Beyond the cultivated land on the ranch were many varieties of beautiful cactus. The most outstanding were the stands of Saguaro, 150 to 200 year old, and in June big fragrant ivory blossoms burst forth from the arms of the stately cactus.

I drove the family to nearby towns to shop, most often to Cuernavaca, actually known worldwide as "The City of Eternal Spring" due to its outstanding climate. This city is considered an excellent place to live and attracts people who seek a sunny place and fresh mountain air.

There is a large cultural community and many tourist activities available. The city, founded seven centuries ago, sits a mile high in the Sierra Madre Mountains. The Pyramid of Teopanzolco is nearby. Cuernavaca is a modern tropical city that hosts many scientific research institutes, and an industrial park with over one hundred industries. There are seventeen universities and extensions of the National University in Mexico City. It has also been established as an international learning center for Mexico's language, culture and history. There are many outdoor markets, some with lovely traditional handicrafts, antique bazaars and exotic plant and flower nurseries. During Holy Week, there is a fair in the city, which lasts two weeks. The fair typically offers a variety of commercial products and handicrafts, as well as cultural, popular and musical events.

I was allowed to bring Johnnie along for a couple of days. He liked the face painting, the prizes for the little games of skill along the midway, and seeing all the costumed characters. He was a good boy and we all enjoyed having him along.

After the fair, we usually went to town and Perla and the girls shopped for clothes, shoes, toys and jewelry. Perla purchased household goods. They loved their fun shopping trips. I carried their purchases and kept them in the van so they could shop unencumbered by bags. We always enjoyed a meal at a gourmet restaurant of their choice before heading home. The one they most enjoyed had fine Mexican food and a mariachi band that played while customers were dining.

The family was very appreciative of me and I loved being in the country. The job was a huge change in pace, but it was good for me at the time. I was ready for a job with very little stress for awhile. I was able to relax and start to think about what I wanted to do in the future.

Marlena and I talked about what we might do next and I told her the job wasn't going to be long term but explained to her that it was alright for awhile. I told her that the country seemed like a great place to live.

Marlena was glad that I had a well paying job. She was so used to me being gone that she didn't seem to mind the times that I had stay on the ranch or be gone with the family overnight.

There was a bunkhouse on the ranch so I stayed there returning home on scheduled days off. I was always asked to be present if the family was entertaining or if they were off the ranch for any reason.

In early fall in Cuernavaca, there was the "Fair of the Ceramics" which lasted a whole week. People came together from communities to exhibit their pottery. These potters were true artisans and their pottery was unusual in color and design. Their customers came from the city and paid good prices for the pottery.

Cathedral in Cuernavaca

The markets offered a wide selection of groceries, fresh vegetables, fruits and meat. Many open-air restaurants in courtyards dotted the neighborhoods I always enjoyed our trips there. It was about a 45-minute drive from the ranch.

Back home there were also social events the family wished to attend, including Sunday dinners with friends or picnics. Birthdays were celebrated in their circle, adults as well the children. These usually consisted of a buffet of Mexican fare, games for the children, cake for all and always a piñata for the celebrant.

Dances were held every Saturday night at the local community hall. These were adult functions and I drove Gustavo and Perla and sometimes a couple they had invited to join them. I waited discreetly just inside the hall watching. I was still their body guard on these occasions. When the dance was over, I drove them home again. Usually they were a little tipsy and needed a driver.

There were social events all year long in Mexico City as well: theatre, opera, art exhibits and much more. I drove them to the city often. On those visits which included Gustavo, I'd have free time to see Johnnie.

The event the family most enjoyed was the fair on the outskirts of Mexico City. It was very large. There were the usual commercial booths, handcrafted items and flowers exhibited. Many food booths offered an extensive assortment of mouthwatering food. For the children there was a large cubicle where several artists did face painting. There were animal exhibits, carnival rides and games of skill presenting prizes for knocking over bottles or hitting a bull's eye target with an air rifle. Prizes for these usually were inexpensive stuffed toys or a pick of cheap toys in a box. Jugglers entertained, as well as fire-eaters and magicians. Characters on tall stilts delighted the children by tossing candy out of baskets.

Perla allowed me to bring Johnnie. As in Cuernavaca, he was fascinated by the colors of the midway, the riot of neon ornamenting the displays and especially looked forward to his cotton candy. Perla and her family were very good to Johnnie and enjoyed having him along. I brought Hugo occasionally, but he was a little younger and not able to fully enjoy the festivities. His little legs got tired of walking so far and he still took naps so he tired by afternoon.

In the middle of the huge fairgrounds was a track. Horse racing took place the entire time the fair was open. These races drew big crowds to watch the finest racehorses in all of Mexico. The purses were worth thousands as betting was very popular. The jockeys were the best and they were famous. Paparazzi followed the jockeys there like they do movie stars in the U.S. Newspapers reported on the horse races, jockeys, wins and losses and related news all year long.

Gustavo's family loved the big rodeo above all the other events. It ran one week during the fair and was the national championship for Mexico. The best ropers, bulldoggers, bronco riders and bull riders competed.

Events like 'wild horse race' were popular too. Wild horses were turned into the arena and teams of cowboys tried to rope one, settle it down somehow, get a saddle on it and one of the team had to get on the horse and try to ride it. These cowboys were young, rough and tough.

Several favorite tactics were used by these cowboys to get the wild horses to cooperate.

One cowboy bit down on a horse's ear and grabbed his nose with his hand and kept the horse from breathing so they could put a blanket and saddle on him. The cowboy then allowed him to breathe, but kept the pressure on while the other member of the team tried to quickly put blanket and saddle on the wild thing and then mount him.

Gustavo's family and I all thought the bull riding was the most exciting event. The bulls were enormous. Mexican steers with full horns were some of the best bucking stock available. It was such a show to watch when the chute opened and a cowboy sat atop one of these leaping, whirling bulls, for the few seconds necessary to qualify. The rodeo clowns were real professionals and saved many bull riders' lives. It occurred to me our jobs were similar: we were both protecting by diverting danger. Even at events such as the fair, I couldn't let my guard down. All the while I was watching everything.

At fair time after the horse racing and rodeo, when darkness fell, there was a spectacular fireworks display. It featured the newest, best fireworks available at the time. The whole sky lit up and the cannons roared as they shot the big rockets into the night sky. Surprisingly, Gustavo could hardly wait for this part of the evening.

Chapter 28

After the fair, school started and things on the ranch returned to normal.

Often on weekends, Perla and the girls had me drive them out along a main road in the outlying areas of Mexico City, wherever they were drawn to. Even though I found it strange, they went where they had a sense that fatal auto accidents had taken place. I was instructed to park the van and they would get out and walk and then stop and sit down and go into a trance. They rubbed their hands together and then made a throwing motion as if they were casting something around them. When I asked what they were doing, they explained that people had been killed in accidents on the road and they were freeing their spirits by sending spiritual light. The spirit was then able to leave and find rest where it was supposed to go. Again I thought it odd, but in my country many believe in ESP and supernatural activities.

On one of these outings, I noticed that the oldest daughter, Tia, sounded like she was talking a different language than Spanish and I asked about it. Perla explained that she was a spiritess and when they were at a place on the road where an accident had been, Tia sometimes went into a trance, and could then speak the language of the dead, no matter what language it happened to be. She was speaking German that day and another time I was surprised to hear her speaking fluent French. She spoke other languages that were not familiar to me. She had never been schooled in any foreign language. Remembering now, I recall how astonished I was at the time at Tia's ability to speak these languages in her trance.

One day Tia told me to stop all of a sudden while we were traveling. She got out of the van and sat down in a large red ant hill. I jerked open the van door to get her out of there and Perla, said, "Don't worry, she'll be fine."

I told her, "Those ants will bite the hell out of her. The bites may make her sick."

Perla repeated to me, "It's alright, Manuel, they won't even bother her."

My job was to keep everyone from harm and I was really concerned for Tia. But, sure enough, the ants started crawling around on her, even going toward her ears, mouth, nose and all over. She felt nothing. She was in that trancelike state several minutes. Then she made a downward motion with her hands and the ants crawled off and away from her immediately. She got up and walked back to the van.

I just couldn't believe it. The ants didn't bother her at all, no biting, nothing. I started believing and respecting the spirit work they were doing. I talked with them about their religious beliefs and was informed that they still believed a lot of the old Nahuatl religion. This religion is very old, going back to the Mayans. There are still many indigenous people who actually speak Nahuatl dialects. Among this religion's beliefs is that there were four lightning hurling saints. Light seemed to be a part of their religious belief and had special significance to them. They also worshipped a sun god. Oddly enough, these groups of people that believe the older religion do so in combination with Catholicism.

Perla said that the older women from the village had handed down a recipe for a bad potion. It was to be used only if their men treated them badly and didn't stop after warnings from the Priest. If given this potion, the man would be unable to use his brain properly and be fairly useless for life. This may have been an old wives tale, I never knew of anyone given the potion.

Perla believed that she and Tia could talk to the dead. She told me that three Indians and horses were taking care of me from the spirit world so nothing would happen to me. I figured it was true because things happened to me before and after that time which surely could have caused my death, but didn't.

Chapter 29

I fell under Perla's spell very soon after taking my position as a driver for the family, but I resisted the feelings she stirred in me and told myself there would be no romantic relationship between us.

Late in the fall, she told me to pack for a trip and that she wanted me to drive her to Los Hatas Resort in Manzanillo, some 720 kilometers distant. We took several of these trips whenever Perla wished me to drive her. Los Hatas is a popular resort right on the ocean just a few miles out of Manzanillo. The movie "Ten", starring Bo Derek was filmed there. Gustavo was on an extended trip, but there was a nanny to see to the girls and hired hands protecting the ranch while we were gone.

The trip was long so we spent one night on the road. She arranged rooms for each of us at a small hotel. It was not grand but clean and comfortable. They served a nice dinner in a small dining room. We were tired, said goodnight and went to our respective rooms. The trip was pleasant.

When we neared Los Hatas Resort, I could see the splendor of it. From the resort, which is situated on the side of a hill, the view is breathtaking. Palm trees bend and sway on white sand beaches that meet the blue ocean. Buildings are all pure white, with roofs of red round tile. The grounds are ablaze with bougainvillea climbing everywhere and poinsettia hedges lining the driveways. In the center of the large main building there was a courtyard the size of half a city block in which a large inviting swimming pool and outdoor restaurant were situated. The pool was deep blue with white and blue tile lining the entire rim. A myriad of potted trees and flowers graced the courtyard. Large cages containing colorful parrots and macaws dotted the grounds. My satchel held a few art supplies and I was anxious to paint.

Perla went into the lobby while I parked the van. I joined her there and on our way out,

I asked if she had our rooms rented already and she replied, "If it's alright with you, why don't you share my room?" This was not totally unexpected. From time to time, her eyes held mine a moment too

long or her hand rested a fraction of a
minute more than necessary.

In my mind, I thought, Don't go. But
there she was, beautiful and sexy, looking
me right in the eye and wanting me. I did
not hesitate, saying, "I'd be delighted."
There were days that we never left the
room, and had food delivered.

Some people think women get all
emotionally attached to men they have a
relationship with but that men don't. That
may be true some times, but I fell deeply
in love with Perla and had never felt as
relaxed, free and natural with anyone else.
I felt we were soul mates and so did she.
But there was no talking about the two of
us trying to be together. We were both
married and her husband wealthy. She
knew how to enjoy the wealth, too.

Perla said to me right before we
returned home, "You need to buy
something nice for your wife and son, so
let's go to the gift shop." Maybe she felt
guilty. At the gift shop Perla bought my
wife Marlena a beautiful outfit and toys for
the children.

Meanwhile my lovely wife and son
waited at home and since my job took me
away routinely, Marlena probably didn't

dream of the situation that was taking place.

Chapter 30

Gustavo's oldest daughter, Tia, 18, who was also extremely attractive, looked much like Perla. She had a warmth and happiness about her, a sweet personality and an easy smile. She began to flatter me, telling me how handsome I looked, how looking into my eyes made her weak in the knees. These comments just kept coming out of her mouth. It was obvious that she had a crush on me. For the first year I worked for them, she had been shy and then she became braver and braver. She flirted with me all the time and told me she wanted me. When there were other people around, she behaved innocently.

I resisted her advances and told her to think of me only as an employee of the family.

She wore the popular white Mexican blouses with elastic at the neckline. The material could then be pulled down off the shoulders exposing those and a good bit of cleavage. Tia wore her blouses off the shoulders frequently. With these blouses, she wore brightly patterned skirts and sandals.

She wore one of the revealing blouses the day that Perla asked me to drive Tia out for her spiritess work. The rest of the family couldn't go along that day. We went ahead, the two of us. Tia chose a spot for me to park under a shade tree off the main highway on a side road. After I pulled over and shut the car off, she reached for me and put her arms around my neck and said huskily, "You know I want you and I'm a grown woman now." By this time she was pressing against me, her warm breath on my neck. Then she kissed me, one of those kisses I will never forget. I took her in my arms.

I was sure this was her first time but she urged me on. She was surprisingly aggressive and very sexy. Afterwards, she curled up against me and we drank sodas that we had brought for the outing. I thought to myself, "What will I do if she tells any of her family?" Tia seemed to read my mind and assured me that no one would ever know about us.

I told her I hoped she kept that promise because a lot would be at stake for me. At the time I wondered who would kill me, Perla or her husband Gustavo. Fortunately, Tia kept her promise and I avoided being alone with her. I was ashamed of my actions. I was supposed to be her protector and in my heart, I knew it was wrong to even touch her. Then and there I vowed to myself not to touch her again. Tia took it well when I told her how I felt. She promised she fully understood. Opportunities didn't come along again for her and me to be alone after that.

Soon, Tia went away to college, met a boy, and fell madly in love. He was the son of a wealthy business owner and seemed like a nice young man. Gustavo approved heartily. The wealth of the bridegroom's family was solid and they enjoyed a more-than-acceptable social status.

Tia and her young man were married at the Catholic Church in the next little community. Her parents had a big reception at the ranch. Gustavo had a large dance platform built out beyond the patio and they strung lights on poles around it. Extra helpers were hired to help Emily with the food and beverage service.

My wife and I were invited and danced at the wedding party. Tia asked for a dance that evening and told me while we dancing that she would never forget me and that I had been special to her. I told her I was happy for her and that I thought her bridegroom was lucky to have her.

Things went along fairly normal for the remainder of the time I worked at the ranch.

Chapter 31

After working two and a half years for Gustavo and his family, I received a letter with a very promising job offer. Ramon had recommended me to his friend who was Head of Judicial Police for the town of Mexicali. I was granted an interview and offered the position of Chief of Police of Mexicali. It was a busy town just across the border from California. I thought I would like this position.

The job was perfect, considering my background and vast military experience. Some good challenges and the excitement of doing criminal investigations again were just what I needed. Change was good and the prospect of a new life inviting.

When I told my wife Marlena of my job offer, she was very quiet and didn't respond.

I said, "What's wrong honey, don't you want to move to Mexicali? This is a good opportunity for me."

She wrung her hands while telling me, "You have been gone so much Manuel. You have not been here for Hugo and me. I feel we've been neglected."

I stood there stunned, I had no idea she felt that way or that she wouldn't come willingly with me to Mexicali. I could say nothing for a time, then I went over to her and put my arms around her, "Marlena, you never said a thing. I'm so very sorry because I feel you are partly right. My job does take me away too much and I can't blame you for feeling this way, but you know I love you. Please make this move with me and we can start new again."

"No, no, Manuel," she said quietly through tears. "I have a good job now. My mother helps us out and I have no intention of moving with you. I would be worried all the time with you being in law enforcement." I thought she would change her mind and I asked her once again the next morning to move with me so we would make a fresh start, and once again she said no.

It was no surprise since I had been gone too much and she probably felt that my heart wasn't with her and Hugo like it should have been.

Of course I was sorry. I felt terrible. I wanted my family with me and to start out new in Mexicali, but it was not to be. What a failure I felt like. Two marriages down the tube. After we parted, I hoped for time to do some real soul searching

Marlena insisted on a divorce and when I realized I couldn't get her to reconsider, I signed the necessary papers. I knew she would never keep me from seeing my son Hugo and I assured her I would send her money and visit and write Hugo regularly.

I had a long talk with Gustavo and told him that I appreciated his trusting me to be the family body guard and that I had enjoyed the job, too. However, mentioning that my wife and I were getting a divorce didn't seem something I wanted to share with him right then. I explained that I had received a good job offer and felt I should take it.

He knew I missed the type of work I was used to. He said, "Well, Manuel, you have the background for the job and, of course, I don't blame you for accepting the position. We'll sure miss you though."

I asked him if three weeks' notice was enough for him to replace me and he said, "Yes, there is an officer I know that is recently retired and he's available."

I then made plans for the move to Mexicali.

I was able to rent a small house in a nice part of town. The house was white with brown wood trim, door and fence. It had three bedrooms, a nice kitchen and bathroom. I felt lucky to find it.

Perla had me take her to the nearest town for groceries the week before I left. We were still lovers and she made sure that we had time alone. After we got to town we stopped to have a soda in a little courtyard café. She leaned forward, looked at me very seriously and announced "Manuel, I am going to leave Gustavo and come to Mexicali with you. Since you and your wife are getting divorced, you can take me, can't you?"

I put my arms around her. "Perla what are you thinking? What about the girls? Gustavo is going to be raging mad and hurt. He has been able to give you everything you could ever want and you know I'm not a wealthy man."

"I don't care," she said, "I must be with you. Tia has her own home now with a husband to care for her. Ida asked Gustavo and me just last week if we would let her go to the Catholic boarding school in Mexico City for her last two years of high school. With Tia gone, she gets lonesome and wants to be around other girls her own age. She'll be fine, I can visit her often. I'll tell Gustavo I'm leaving after you've been gone a couple weeks."

"Well, you must understand this, my love, I will not be able to provide you with everything you are used to, things that you take for granted here," I said. "You have to think about this and be sure before you come to me in Mexicali."

Perla answered, "Please do not worry, I understand everything."

"Then try to work things out as well as you can with Gustavo," I said. "I'm afraid he'll seek retaliation for me stealing you away. Who could blame him?"

Reaching for my hand, she said, "Don't worry, dear one, I'll handle it. I just found out a month ago that my 'dear husband' has had a mistress in Mexico City for a couple years. I came across a letter from her in his desk drawer. I've had a feeling he had someone, but I looked the other way. Now I will tell him to go to her. I will confront him about my feelings and heartbreak and how he has forced me to distance myself from him."

"Alright but I'm still concerned about Gustavo's reaction. He has been good to me, fully respecting my capabilities while I was body guard for your family. My relationship with Gustavo has been one of mutual trust. I feel bad for cheating with his wife. Perla, I'm not sorry that you and I fell in love, but please understand, my reputation is at stake."

A military connection I still kept probably saved me Gustavo's wrath. My prior superior officer, Juan Carlos, was a friend of Gustavo and he called me and related that he had spent an evening with Gustavo. Over many margaritas and dinner, Juan reminded Gustavo that I had been a fearless soldier as well as a favorite of El Presidente Ecchevaria. He pointed out to Gustavo that the fault could not all be mine. Perla knew she was leaving a life of luxury.

Juan told his friend, "When reality hits, Perla will realize the error in her judgment. Why don't you try to look the other way this one time, Gustavo? Nothing will be gained if you seek revenge. Since she found out about your mistress, she's probably mad, upset and hurt. No doubt her actions are payback at this time."

Evidently Gustavo decided to take no action toward me. My gut feeling was that I might hear from him in the future.

Chapter 32

Perla was nine years older than me, but I didn't care. We were well suited in temperament, interests and sexuality. She treated me very well, rubbed my feet when I came home tired, cooked good meals, and made me feel special. We were very happy together.

As the months went by, however, the life she lived with me was so different, I thought she might be having second thoughts. She was always used to a social status of prominence and they regularly enjoyed the best entertainment in the area. She had a nanny, servants and a cook. When I asked her why she was feeling blue once in awhile, she assured me that she didn't miss her life of luxury and that everything was fine. I took her to visit her children and friends often; usually they met in Mexico City. While she was with her friends, I visited my two boys. These trips were always enjoyable and Perla and I talked, listened to music and sang songs on the drive and she seemed happy.

My position, Chief of Police, was going well. I loved the busy schedule, and the challenges of good detective work necessary to solve difficult cases. My employees numbered ten by now, had respect for me and I was well accepted in the community.

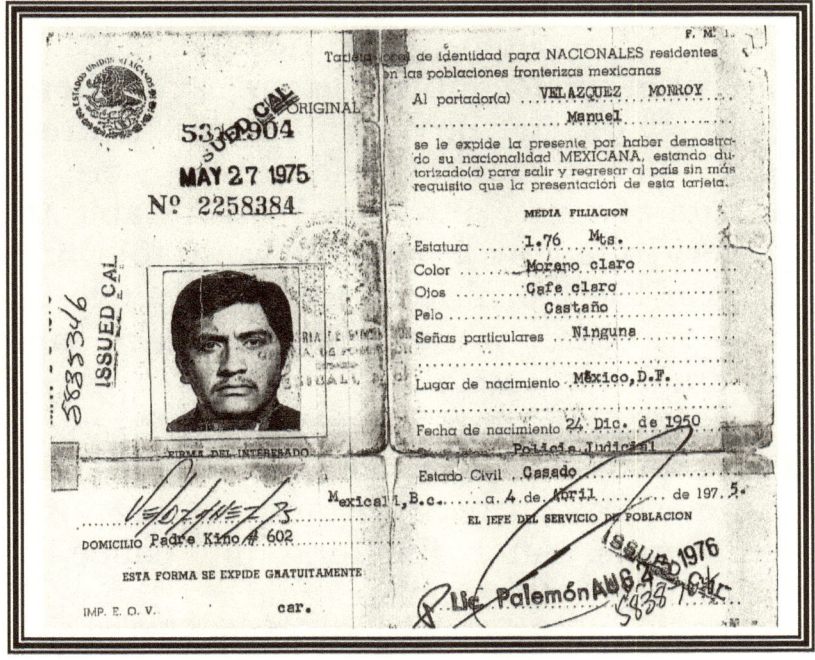

Chapter 33

One morning after driving to town to pick up a telegram, I did a little shopping and stopped at Jaun's Diner for a cup of coffee and to catch up on the latest gossip. Several of the local businessmen met there before work in the morning and shared news. Visits to the coffee shop were a favorite of mine, although I wasn't able to go very often as I usually went to work early in the morning to review paperwork, and prioritize what cases to have my officers investigate.

That morning however, I enjoyed listening to the locals swap their versions of the events of the week and visiting with my friends. After finishing my coffee, I walked up to the cashier, paid my tab and went out and got in my own pickup. I turned on the key and as the engine started, I looked up and there in front of me was a taxi with the door open. A man was walking out of the old rooming house beside the diner and I recognized him immediately. It was none other than "The Monkey," a notorious safe cracking robber. He had robbed the pharmacy, newspaper office, two other local businesses and a few particular residents. His picture was on wanted posters and here he was standing right in front of me.

The Monkey was headed for the taxi and stopped to have a word with someone on the street. I got out of my truck slowly and walked over. Just as he turned around to get into the taxi, I said, "Stop. Don't move. You are under arrest." He acted like he wasn't even going to move and answered, "Alright, alright." Then all of a sudden he turned half way around toward me and I saw a gun in his hand. He shot me point blank. When he fired, people heard the shot and came to see what happened. He put his pistol away, thinking he would escape.

For a couple seconds, I thought I was dead. I had felt a thud in my chest. I started to fall and grabbed the back bumper of the taxi as I went down. After a minute, I realized that I was ok and caught my breath. In my uniform shirt pocket was my metal identification badge, which had stopped the projectile as it crashed into it. The bullet had been going right to my heart, through my coat as well as my shirt when it collided with my ID badge. I had only been stunned.

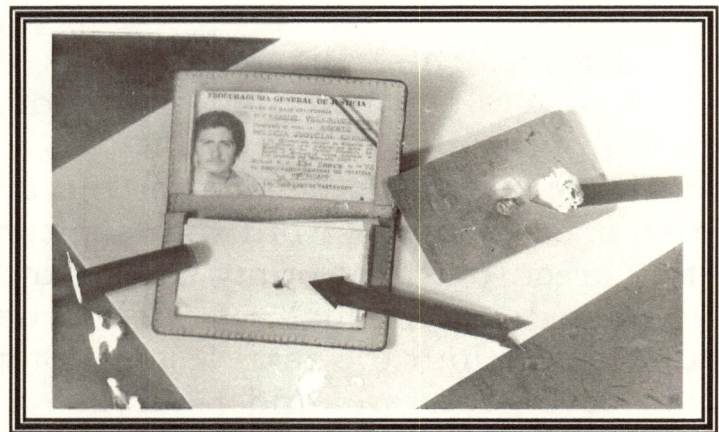

The badge that saved his life

The Monkey must have thought I fell dead, but instead I eased up the back of the taxi, turned around, drew my gun and jumped on back of the car just as the driver was pulling away from the curb. I yelled, "Stop, driver!"

"Monkey, put your hands up or I'll kill you on the spot. Step out of the car and drop your gun on the street."

The taxi stopped and The Monkey saw me standing there pointing a loaded 38 at him. He had never taken his pistol back out of his holster.

The Taxi didn't move because the driver knew I was an officer of the law and witnessed the entire event. The Monkey stepped out and dropped his gun onto the street. I quickly grabbed him, threw him up against the Taxi and handcuffed him. I kicked him into the back of my police car. I drove him to the station and we jailed him.

In The Monkey's robberies, he left pieces of paper, insults and challenges to police officers, especially naming Chief Salvador, the prior, who had arrested him previously. The Monkey had served a ten-year sentence and must have gotten out just before he committed the recent safe cracking robberies.

When I got home, Perla had already heard about the shooting and she was understandably frightened but glad I was still alive. We celebrated that weekend. We went out, drank some good tequila, had an intimate dinner and went dancing.

I was thankful to be alive. Perla was an exciting, intelligent woman and a pleasure to be with. In the back of my mind, however, I always knew the cold reality of the situation. This woman would not be mine for long.

Chapter 34

Time went by and things were pretty normal, but then I noticed that Perla was having more times when she felt blue. We tried to make the best of it, but I knew our lifestyle did not please her. Perla treated me lovingly yet she just wasn't happy any longer. She had never settled into life in Mexicali.

Worrying about it didn't help me any and after thinking about the situation a couple weeks, I knew what I must do.

One night we were lying in bed almost asleep and I said, "Perla, I love you and most of all I want you to be happy. You don't seem happy even as hard as I know you have tried. Go back home where you have friends and family. I understand. We'll get together whenever we can."

She started to sob, "Oh, my love, I'm so sorry, but I think you are right. I've tried so very hard, but I just don't fit in. Mexicali does not suit me and life here is too different. Please promise me you'll see me whenever you can."

I held her close and whispered in her ear, "Of course I will. You gave up so much for me and tried so hard to make it work. I'll always be here for you, if you need me."

She left the next week and we stayed in touch. If either of us had a problem or crises in our lives, we contacted the other and sometimes got together routinely to visit. Interestingly, the following year, Gustavo begged Perla to come back to him. He told Perla that she was the only woman he had ever loved and that the mistress had never meant anything to him. She returned to him after he reassured her that he would never stray again. He completely forgave her too. Gustavo knew she had left me and didn't think of me as a threat. He seemed to understand Perla and me talking to each other occasionally if we had rough times. By this time, we were friends not lovers.

Chapter 35

My military career had never been boring and neither was the position of police chief. I have shared some of my recollections about drug trafficking and drug busts that took place during my military service. In Mexicali, I came across a new method for transporting drugs.

Sometimes I went on patrol. One late afternoon I went with Carlos, one of my officers, to patrol a section of highway that led to the border. This, of course, is one of the routes used by drug traffickers.

I liked Carlos and had great respect for him. He was tall, handsome and muscular, 35 years old. Also he was fast on his feet, intelligent and cunning. He had been on the force for 15 years, was an excellent shot and reacted instantly in an emergency situation. Traffic was moving along nicely, nothing looked suspicious, and we were having an uneventful afternoon. We were talking about police business and the news of the day. A stalled Ford Taurus was stopped along the highway and we pulled up behind it.

The car looked like it had had some hard miles, but it and the occupants seemed very ordinary.

Two young women were evidently trying to change a flat tire. They said they were students going to visit an aunt in San Diego. One was tall and thin, and had dyed her hair a reddish color. The other was rather short and had black hair.

We ran a quick check on the car and saw that their papers were in order and asked: "Ladies, can we give you a hand here? This is a busy highway and it would be prudent to get you back on the road."

They both answered at once, "Oh, yes, please." Then the red headed one added, "We'd be so grateful."

The spare tire had been removed from the car along with the jack. The flat tire was lying on the side of the road and I offered, "While Carlos puts the spare on, could you open the trunk and I'll put your flat and tools in for you."

They exchanged nervous looks, which I noticed but didn't think much of. The short girl replied, "Yes, that would save time, too, I'll open it up." She opened the trunk and I put the spare in and left it open because Carlos was about to put the tools away too. There were several cases of refried beans in cardboard boxes in the trunk. I asked, "Are you taking the refried beans to your aunt?"

The red head answered, "We get them for our aunt and cousins. They love this brand and can't buy them in San Diego."

Something was bothering me and then I realized it was the cans. They were not all sitting upright. Some were upside down, not the way they should have been packed in their cardboard cases with tops up.

I reached over and picked one up, then noticed the short girl quickly walked around to the front of the car. I said "Carlos, grab her, we may have a drug situation here. She may be armed."

At the instant I told him that, I had reached out and grabbed the arm of the red head and told her not to move. I bent her arm behind her so she couldn't reach her purse or anything else.

I knew the moment I picked up the can that it wasn't heavy enough for refried beans. The cans were sealed though and we had to open one.

Carlos searched the short woman, cuffed her to the door handle of the car and came back to assist me. He pulled out his knife and immediately opened the can.

It was stuffed with a couple plastic bags of marijuana. There were quite a lot of cans so it was a sizeable bust.

I put cuffs on the redhead. Carlos helped me put them in the police car and he drove the Taurus back to the station.

Upon interrogating the women, we found out that they worked with their boyfriends, who grew the marijuana in their home. It was a big operation and we were able to bust them that very evening.

Manuel (Foreground) booking the bad guys

We knew if they didn't hear from the women that the drugs had reached their destination, the men would bolt. They were in the house when our teams surrounded it. We used a loudspeaker to inform them they would be wise to come out with their hands up. They did.

These two had been very innovative. Elaborate lighting was used to grow the plants and they had even installed air conditioning. The electric supply had been dangerously tampered with to bypass the meter to avoid detection from telltale bills.

We seized the marijuana that was already packaged for sale. There were 20 pounds packaged for sale and all the plants. Bright government notices reading, "Condemned/Keep Out" were placed on the house and Carlos and I drove back to the station in their new black Suburban, which would now be government property, as would the home and all contents.

Since we worked with the drug enforcement officers in San Diego, we apprised them of our bust and gave them the names of the proposed buyer of this shipment. The men resisted giving that information, but fortunately the women had never been in trouble, were scared, and told us the name and location of the drop we needed. Again, time was of the essence because the shipment was expected at a certain time and the buyers would know trouble had befallen the women if they didn't show.

The next day, we received a call from the officers in San Diego thanking us. The buyers of the shipment had been arrested; they were also in possession of sizeable quantities of meth and cocaine. The case against them would be sufficient to put them away for some time.

Chapter 36

A few months later, we had been on an assignment to investigate a possible drug dealing operation in a neighborhood not far out of town. Cannabis was showing up in this neighborhood. We had received phone calls from citizens who had noticed young people smoking pot in the park, in parked cars and in the parking lots of local eateries. Also, cannabis was found in too many routine traffic stops.

Large shipments of marijuana arrive usually in boats or container ships in nearby ports and are then distributed by traffickers. Carlos had been given the detail of patrolling the neighborhood in question. He returned one afternoon and buzzed me asking if I had time to meet with him. I said, "Sure, come on in. Have a chair, what's going on? We've been so busy we haven't even gotten away for lunch in ages."

"Oh, I know," he replied as he took off his hat, wiped his brow and sat down. "Well", he said, "I think I've got a real lead on the distribution of marijuana in the neighborhood I'm investigating."

"You aren't going to believe it. They are using bicycles. I kept concentrating on all the cars, occupants, comings and goings of the families, trying to find a pattern of suspicious activity. Today, I was parked partially concealed by a large tree on a side street when a family on bicycles rode along about a half block away. There was a man and woman with two children, a girl about ten and a boy that looked eight. All were riding along, talking and laughing and enjoying themselves. I was thinking what a nice family when they drove into a driveway then parked the bikes. The dad got off and told the kids, 'You stay right here and mind the bikes, we'll just be a minute.' The woman then got off her bike and they both got packages from saddle type bags on their bikes and took them to the side entrance of the home. He knocked a couple times and a man answered the door He accepted the packages and handed an envelope to the cyclist, said, 'Thanks' and went back inside. I'm pretty sure it was marijuana. My instinct was to immediately stop them for questioning and search them but I noticed out of the corner of my eye that a dark colored newer car was parked down the block. My concern was that it likely might be a look out for their protection. They will no doubt keep delivering and we can set up a proper arrest with enough officers. We better have a matron along to assist with the children."

"Well, you're right Carlos, I wouldn't have ever guessed they'd be peddling this amount of drugs on bicycles," I remarked as I sat back in my chair and laughed. "We'll set something up right away and nab them. You are right about needing a matron along. The children don't need to be scared and we'll handle it so that doesn't happen."

Two days later, we went undercover with search warrants in unmarked cars to the site where Carlos had seen the activity. We drove around several blocks and into the adjoining neighborhood, and then parked a few blocks apart. We had radios and brought the matron with us. Backup officers were in regular cars a mile away to call. We waited and waited and nothing, no bicycles with adults. A few children glided by but that was all. "Well, shall we wait longer?" Carlos asked.

"Yes," I said, "I just have a feeling they will be along."

Sure enough, here they came, just as Carlos described. The four rode along looking like a happy family on an outing. A car pulled up just before they started bicycling up the block. We figured it was their back up. The timing was precise and Carlos said it was the same car as before. We waited until they pedaled along and then they pulled in and stopped three houses from where we were parked. We quickly called our officers to nab the car.

The man got off his bicycle, and as before instructed the children to stay with the bikes, the woman then got off hers. He and the woman took packages out of their respective saddle bags. The two walked up to the door and knocked. A woman opened the door, smiled and said, "Just a minute." We wanted to arrest her too so we moved stealthily but quickly over to the house, ducking around shrubs and keeping out of sight until she came out with the envelope. We came around the side of the house, weapons drawn and I said, "DON'T MOVE."

Carlos yelled: "You, too, lady, don't even think about shutting that door or we'll shoot right through it before you can get out of the way."

Our backup was immediately behind us and two of them immediately cuffed the man and woman delivering the pot. Carlos grabbed the woman at the door. I covered him with my weapon. Three more officers watched the front door to the home and entered. We wanted to make sure no one else was in the house. Another officer was posted at the back door.

The look out, in the car down the block, had already been arrested, cuffed, and placed in one of the police cars under guard. The matron ushered the children down the block telling them that there was danger in the area and they went quietly with her. She placed them in one of the police cars with her. The parents were charged with possession and delivery of marijuana and later given jail sentences at their hearing. Fortunately, an aunt was able to care for the children.

The main object of Mexico's drug enforcement program was, of course, to arrest the drug traffickers who were the organizers of the whole delivery plan. This didn't happen right away, but after the man and his wife had been in jail for a few months, the two decided to cooperate with the law and give up the names of the traffickers. They were taking a chance because if anyone in this drug trafficking organization found out they had named traffickers, their lives would have been in danger. It was decided that they should serve more of their sentence, and not be freed until the traffickers had been arrested, tried and jailed. Thus, danger would be less for the couple.

Carlos was congratulated on his good work and we closed that case and went back to our ongoing investigations and routine arrests.

Chapter 37

My work always kept me quite busy, but it was difficult without Perla. My little house felt so empty, no one to share my life with. Meals are not enjoyable when you have to dine alone. Also missing was a woman to hold in my arms. Nights were painfully long and lonely.

I enjoyed my trips to Mexicali to visit my children. I wrote and called them regularly and sent money for their care. Both of my ex-wives had new husbands by this time. They were good responsible men who treated my children well. I wanted to have a good relationship with the boys so I kept in contact often.

Carmen, who saved my life during the massacre in 1968, called regularly and asked if I would bring my little boys by so she could see them, as she missed the company of children. The boys and I visited her routinely and she loved my kids and they loved her. She made cookies in shapes of animals for them. They always looked forward to seeing what master-pieces of sugary treats she had waiting for them. Most of the time, we just sat in Carmen's kitchen and talked. Sometimes if she needed groceries, we took her shopping. Other times, if the boys and I were seeing something special like a museum exhibit, we took Carmen along.

Carmen meant a lot to me. She had become a mother and grandmother figure. I didn't have a relationship with my own mother. I am sure Carmen thought of us as her family too. She didn't get to see her family often so she doted on us.

During summer and school vacations I brought the boys home and spent fun times with them. They enjoyed playing together and were cute and animated little fellows.

When the school year began again, I put in a lot of extra hours since I was still living by myself. There was plenty of work to do. I most enjoyed the investigations of criminal cases. Since I had a good background in this type of work from my military service, I became quite an accomplished detective.

My boss, Head of the Judicial Police, called me in and informed me that I was to attend a roundtable meeting in San Diego for five days. I was pleased for the change in scenery and always enjoyed the city. Meetings had been scheduled with Mexican police officers from several of the border towns and United States police officers from the other side of the border. The agenda included ways we could work more effectively together. We needed faster, more comprehensive information about criminal sightings, activities and ways we could share information, especially in child kidnapping and drug trafficking cases.

The roundtable was a working conference and we got right to work. We explored methods of communication and discussed proper protocol. A plan was instituted to have special hot line phones installed. We all agreed to work together and to have another roundtable discussion to see how everything was working and to explore additional methods for fast apprehension of criminals, etc.

Chapter 38

The second of the meetings took place a month later in Los Angeles. It was especially hot that week.

After the meetings finished for the day, I returned to my motel and took a shower.

I decided to change into my swimsuit and strolled out to the pool. After swimming several laps, I got out and stretched out on a lounge chair. When the waiter came by, I bought a Corona and enjoyed the afternoon.

I was about half done with my beer when a young woman got out of the pool and walked over , "Is this other lounge chair taken?"

I looked up. She was so stunning she took my breath away. I quickly composed myself and smiled, saying, "NO, by all means, help yourself. I'm here alone."

"Well, handsome, are you single then?"

"Why, yes, I sure am."

"Great," she said as she stretched out on the lounge chair and put on her sun glasses. Without obviously staring, I saw she was a tan, bronze beauty, her dark

hair pulled back in a graceful knot. She
didn't look Mexican and I couldn't guess
her nationality.

I saw the waiter nearby. "Can I buy
you a beer or something?"

"Yes, the Corona looks good." The
waiter brought the beer. We sipped our
drinks and enjoyed the sun.

I introduced myself and asked her
name. "Yadira," she replied, and then
smiled a sweet smile. When she did, her
eyes sparkled. They were beautiful and
brown, almost almond shaped. I've never
seen such eyelashes. I first thought they
were false, but they weren't. Her red bikini
did not cover much of her body, which was
pretty damn sensational.

She turned to me and asked: "Where
are you from?"

"Mexicali, Mexico, I'm in town for
business meetings."

"Oh, you speak very good English."

"Thanks, how about you, where do
you call home?" I asked.

She chuckled and replied, "Panama
City, I'm here for a seminar on cardiac
care. I'm a nurse specializing in that field."
After a little more banter, I asked if she'd
have dinner with me.

She thought a minute and then answered, "Sure, Italian sound good." I told her about a great place I knew called "Venezias".

Yadira seemed to like me. We enjoyed a comfortable visit and our beer. I liked everything about her. She was attractive but also had an air of self-confidence that intrigued me. I had never met a woman that was so self-assured. No helpless lass here. We agreed to meet in the lobby at seven that evening as we both wanted time to rest, shower and dress.

I would have taken her to any restaurant she asked. The prospect of spending the evening with this woman put me in a mood of happy excitement. It would be interesting to see how the night might progress. She was mysterious and sexy. I thought of her all afternoon.

I entered the lobby that evening, trying my best to appear cool and relaxed. Yadira was already there. I appreciated her being on time. So many women are always late and I detest that. She wore a stunning white dress with a pair of sexy white heels. The dress was low cut. A slit up one side of the skirt allowed a view of well-proportioned, bronze legs. She had taken her hair down and pulled one side up in back of her ear with a mother of pearl clasp, letting the other side fall over her shoulder. As I helped her into the car, I discerned the light, floral scent of her perfume. "You look lovely," I whispered in her ear. I had chosen a white short-sleeved shirt, Mexican style, not tucked in. These are cooler and more comfortable for a warm evening. My slacks were casual khaki pressed with sharp creases. Clothes are important to me. Maybe some of the military attitudes instilled about our uniforms stuck. We always had crisp, clean uniforms with creases and were told that anything less would be sloppy and unacceptable.

Yadira liked the bar I had chosen and we talked, relaxed and got acquainted a little more. Over a glass of wine we both felt more comfortable. Yadira took a sip and looked over at me, leaned across the table and cooed, "You are very handsome, I'm so glad we met at the pool."

Pleased, I answered, "I would have been bored this evening watching television in my room. This evening is most enjoyable. I feel like I've known you longer than this few hours."

"Me too," she said, "I didn't think I would be having a lovely evening like this either."

After finishing our wine, we set off for the Italian restaurant. It was a beautiful night, warm with just a gentle breeze. I drove slowly so we could enjoy the night air.

Upon arriving, we walked slowly toward the restaurant and I couldn't resist nuzzling the back of Yadira's neck. She giggled. We ordered Chianti and took our time looking over the menu. We savored our meals, and reminisced about our backgrounds and families.

After we had lingered over dinner, Yadira said, "We probably should be getting back." The waiter came by with the check, and we walked out to the car and drove back.

When we walked into the lobby, she stopped and very close to my ear said, "Why don't you give me 20 minutes and come to my room for a nightcap."

I looked down at her and smiled. "I'll be there."

I waited a half an hour. She met me at the door wearing a teal silk teddy with a matching short robe over the top. She was stunning in every way, from her perfectly painted hot pink toenails to her hair, clean and smelling wonderful. She had a bottle of champagne chilling and poured us each a glass. I'm not at all fond of champagne, but I drank it anyway.

Soft music was playing in the background, the kind of music meant for a romantic evening.

We visited a little, but when she got up to pour a second glass of champagne, I reached for her and said. "Let's dance." We did dance, for awhile. Then I took her in my arms and gave her a long, gentle kiss and we danced slowly but directly into the bedroom.

I kept telling myself not to hurry, to take my time. I wanted to make the experience last as long as possible.

It was a great night. The passion came quickly and was exhilarating for us both. Later, lying next to each other, we shared how we both felt quite comfortable, especially considering this was our first time together.

I had meetings the next day and Yadira had to attend her seminar. I was tired at the end of the day and decided to take a dip in the pool. She was already swimming and I dove in and came up right next to her. We swam and then decided to get out and dry off. We sat in the lounge chairs and ordered margaritas.

"I want you to know that I really enjoyed last night, our drinks, dinner and everything," I said.

She said, "Yes, last night was special. Tonight, I want to treat you to dinner." She told me about a good seafood place nearby. We agreed to meet at 6:00 pm, and again she was right on time.

She opened up even more in our conversations the second evening. She had been married for five years to a man who just recently told her he wanted a divorce. It wasn't a complete surprise, but her pride was wounded. She hadn't worked through the negative emotions of the breakup. I could tell from the troubled look on her face.

As much as I was trying to be reassuring, I was annoyed that she was one minute loving and fun and the next melancholy. That evening, however, we did again share passion and togetherness. Holding her in my arms, I knew she appreciated the comfort of a warm, attentive body. Always glad to help, I thought to myself as I drifted off to sleep.

We woke up lazily; still close together, her back to me and my arm around her. The smell of her hair and the youthful curves of her body so pleasant, I could have gladly stayed in bed with her the entire day. But she stirred and kissed me gently, then got out of bed as she said, "I have to get ready and go, I have a plane to catch today."

"Alright, honey," I answered, "Go ahead and shower first, I'll order coffee and rolls for us." I ordered room service and we enjoyed our last bit of time together. I told her that she was really special to me, and I hoped we could see each other again soon.

She said she loved being with me, but couldn't enter into a new relationship until she worked through her anger and frustration. I understood, having been divorced myself. I advised her to go home, work on finalizing her divorce, and when she felt like seeing me again, all she had to do was write or call. She told me she had a friend in Mexicali and maybe would get in touch with me if she got to town. I said, "Great, just let me know."

A week after I got home, this letter arrived:

Manuel:

If you would like to share some seconds, minutes, hours and more time, visit a Panamanian (female) who is very sad and who probably cannot offer you a moment's happiness. But if you could give the best you have of feelings and desires in these moments I would love to see you.

I don't know how much time must pass for me to forget our being together.

Last night I was beloved in your arms.

You can imagine what happened when I arrived home. My feelings of well-being are already suffering now, thinking of you. If you desire my sad company for the benefit of we two, please write. I am going to use all of my strength and my self-discipline and forget everything that has happened in this marriage. I have already signed the divorce demand; God desires to give me my liberty. Manuel, for me you are not a stranger, I feel as though I've known you forever. I'm arriving in Mexicali next Saturday.

I miss you,
Yadira

I phoned her right away and told her I would take her out when she came to town.

On that Saturday, Yadira called me when she got to her friend Lupe's home. We made plans for that very evening. I met her friend Lupe and then escorted Yadira to my car.

Again, she was impeccably dressed. She wore a pink, nearly backless sundress. Her hair was caught up high on her head. On her feet were high heels with ankle straps. She didn't need a lot of makeup. This girl was a natural beauty.

We had a great evening. She liked the sea bass, and we enjoyed the band. I asked her if she would like to have a nightcap at my place. She replied, "Yes, I don't have to go back to Lupe's. I told her I probably would spend the night with you."

"I'm glad; since tomorrow is Sunday, we can sleep in and relax".

At my place, we relaxed with a couple of drinks and talked awhile. Then I put some music on and after a couple songs took her hand and pulled her up to dance. She was an excellent dancer; no matter what I did, she fluidly followed my every step. Again, she was self-assured and I thought to myself, "This woman could be a fantastic wife if she could just move past the emotional damage of her divorce."

Yadira still said she felt wounded and wronged by her ex-husband who never gave her any credit for being a good wife or for working during the entire marriage. She felt she had contributed quite a lot to the marriage in many ways. Her job as cardiac care nurse paid very well and she was frugal, handing most of her wages over to her husband. She said she had always willingly cooked gourmet meals and graciously entertained her husband's friends and business associates. I told her that it was perfectly normal to feel this anger and that only time would take away the hurt. She appreciated my understanding.

As for myself, I was glad to be in the company of such a beautiful, sexy woman even if it was for only a short time.

Yadira had to return to Panama the following day. I drove her back to Lupe's house and told her she was very dear to me. "Let me know if you can come back to Mexicali again soon," I said.

"I'll call you," she said. We kissed goodbye and parted.

From then on, my thoughts were of Yadira much of the time. My life as a bachelor seemed worse having been with her and remembering how it was; such a pleasure to have her beside me to cuddle with when I woke up in the morning.

Three weeks later, just after I returned from visiting my children, I got a call from Yadira. She planned to fly in the following week. I told her, "I look forward to seeing you. I've missed you so much. I'll pick you up at the airport and we can decide where you would like to go to dinner."

At the airport she came into my arms immediately and almost clung to me. We drove to a nightspot that I heard had live music and excellent steaks. The music was good so we decided to enjoy it, dancing awhile.

We later moved into the restaurant for a late dinner. We laughed and enjoyed our wine. The steaks were as good as I had been told.

We caught up on what had happened in each other's lives since our last meeting.

Yadira had been busy at work and had moved into her own flat in Panama City. It was a lot closer to the clinic where she worked. Her husband kept their home and gave her a cash settlement per the terms of their divorce. She didn't feel she could afford to make payments on a house, let alone see to the maintenance, yard work, or upcoming repairs. She told me, "I am enjoying settling into my new place. It's cozy and since I'm just renting I don't feel tied down."

I talked about my recent trip to visit the boys and how much fun we'd had. I then said, "Work has been busy as usual, but I don't think you want to hear any of the details. Most of the cases are interesting, but just aren't going to make good dinner conversation."

She laughed and answered, "Well, you know best, but another time I would love to hear more about your work."

"No problem," I answered, "we'll talk."

Dessert was brought to the table on a tray by the waiter. After looking over all the tempting sweets, we settled on chocolate sundaes.

We were full and relaxed and decided to take a walk for several blocks in the night air before heading home. I thought, "What a perfect night," as I put my arm around Yadira.

We strolled slowly, admiring the stars and city lights, stopping occasionally to enjoy the view. She leaned close to me, putting her head on my shoulder and murmured, "Manuel, I wish this night would last forever."

"Me, too," I whispered in her ear as I took her in my arms and held her close.

It was late when we got back to my house. I knew I was falling in love with her. By this stage of my life, I knew the difference between lust and true love. The night was memorable. In my arms, Yadira shared my desire for yet more intimacy.

The next morning I held her to me. "Darling, I care for you more all the time. Are you going to be with me when your divorce is final?"

She was quiet for just a couple moments too long and then said "I'm sorry, I just don't think I can be that involved yet. You know I love you. But everything is up in the air. My job takes so much energy especially since I've gotten the promotion I wanted. Moving here and starting a new job again now would be tough."

My disappointment came over me in the form of actual physical pain in my chest and it took me a few minutes to answer. "I understand, but this is it for me. I am falling in love with you and cannot bear for us to be apart. If we can't be together after your divorce, I can't see you anymore."

She started to cry and said, "I just need more time."

I held her and said as tenderly as I could, "I can't see you once a month or so. It is too hard for me. I want and need someone here with me all the time. I want a wife. I will always care for you, but I can't continue like this."

As we lay there, thoughts swirled in my mind. "Why can't life be easier? Loving someone shouldn't have to be so complicated. I don't want to hurt her." I felt a tear drop onto my chest and could feel her sobs.

"I'm sorry," she said again, still crying softly, "can't we at least be friends?"

As we lay there, I patted her back. "Of course, Yadira, but we can't be together like we have been unless it's for good." We parted, clinging, lingering over our goodbyes and kissing one last time. I drove her to the airport and was miserable.

She was in my thoughts constantly after that day. I missed her badly, but I knew I had made the right choice for both of us. It would have been even more heart breaking if more time went by. There was a part of Yadira that seemed to want freedom and the single life. She called once in awhile but was still unwilling to make any kind of commitment. My feeling was strong that when I love someone, I want to be with her. Despite the yearning, Yadira and I were not meant to be together.

Regret & Sadness Reflected

Chapter 39

My job was still demanding with plenty of cases to work on which distracted me. Very soon, my time and energy was spent in an unusual robbery.

One of our most established and largest banks was robbed and we were all working as hard and fast as we could to investigate everything, every lead, trying to solve this crime.

We first interviewed the teller at length. She related that an hour after the bank opened on a Wednesday morning, a well-dressed young man walked up to her and said. "Good morning."

She smiled and said, "Yes it is, thank you."

"I need to make a withdrawal," he said and handed her a piece of paper the exact size of a withdrawal slip. There was a note written in large letters that said, "I'm going to hand you a bank envelope, put all the paper money in your drawer in it."

She did that and he told her in a low voice, "Walk over to the next window and fill one of your own bank bags with the paper money from that drawer. That teller is occupied at a desk with a customer so hurry. Speak to no one, you are being watched by two men with loaded guns."

Before continuing, she told us, "This guy stared right into my eyes. His eyes were cold and calculating, and he didn't raise his voice right away. But soon he began to talk faster and louder."

Afraid for her life, she did exactly as she was told. She handed the two bags across the counter to the robber who ordered, "Now let me into the safe deposit box room and remember you are being watched. Make it quick."

She accompanied him to the safety deposit box room and he told her to wait for him, not to move or alert anyone. The robber had obviously rented a couple safety deposit boxes prior. He came out very quickly and asked the teller "Is the vault open now?" "Yes," she said.

"OK, walk in; fill three business size bags with large bills and if anyone asks what you are doing, say, 'Just taking care of a business account.'"

"When you come out, hand them to me. I'll put them in my brief case and leave. You are to do nothing, or say anything to anyone for 20 minutes. Just go on as usual and stall if you need to as you will still be covered by the armed lookouts."

The teller told us then what she had told the investigator who was first on the scene, "I was scared and didn't know what to do. I was shaking and could hardly talk. I went to the restroom to compose myself and to while away some of the minutes, then when the time was up, I went right to the bank president's office and alerted him."

At this juncture of our interrogation of the teller, I said, "Excuse us for a minute, please." My partner and I stepped out of the room and discussed whether the teller might be an accomplice. We wondered why she couldn't have pushed the alarm button or alerted someone. But, of course, she did say the robber warned her of the armed lookouts. It was going to be necessary to finish the interviews of all the bank employees before we could figure things out. We walked back in, thanked the teller and told her to contact us immediately if she thought of anything else.

The bank president was questioned next. He was a tall man, dressed in a dark suit, and carried himself with authority. When the robbery took place he had been

working in his office with the door closed
and had also been on the phone. I asked if
he thought the teller could have been an
accomplice. The older man leaned forward
in his chair, put both his hands flat down
on the desk, stared hard at me and said:
"No, her security check was completely
clean and she has worked here for seven
years. I don't believe she was involved at
all."

Levi and I continued interrogations of
the other bank employees. One young
man, a loan officer, who had been with the
bank five years, gave us our only useful bit
of information.

He seemed shy and stood without
taking the chair offered him. Levi asked if
he recalled anything at all unusual about
the day of the robbery.

"Well, yes. I've been thinking about
the robbery and remembered something,"
he said. "A guy came in wearing a suit and
tie that morning. He casually walked over
and engaged the guard in a conversation.
They talked for awhile and seemed to
know each other. I didn't pay much
attention because I was waiting on a
customer."

The young man stopped talking and
looked at us questioningly.

"Go on," I said, "We appreciate your help."

"Well, maybe it was a ploy to take the guard's attention away from his duties. Since it all happened very fast, the security guard wouldn't have noticed anything amiss."

"Can you give us a description of the man who spoke to the guard?" Levi asked.

"Yes," the young loan officer said, "he was medium height, like five foot, ten inches, and looked about 35 or 40 years old. His hair was light brown, cut short. He wore plain gold rimmed glasses, but I couldn't tell you what color eyes he had."

I said, "Good job, could you look at some mug shots to see if you recognize him?"

"I'd be glad to," he said.

"Thanks, we'll call you soon."

We found out that the robbers had placed a sign right in front of the bank, which was a covered entrance situated off the street several feet. The sign said, "Sorry, bank will be closed for one hour due to an electrical failure." That was why no one else entered the bank during the robbery.

There was only one partial smudged fingerprint found. It was on the demand note first handed to the teller. Absolutely no matches were found to that print. Of course, the bank was full of fingerprints because of the many people in and out touching everything, but none were found matching the one on the note.

The loan officer willingly and patiently viewed the mug shots, but couldn't identify any of the hundreds of pictures we showed him

We knew the robber would no doubt come back for the money in the safe deposit boxes or send someone else with the key and proper ID. But, the lessees of safety deposit boxes are guaranteed complete privacy and anonymity even in Mexico. Besides, no useful fingerprints were found.

After all the hard work investigating this robbery, we still couldn't come up with any solid evidence. Day after disappointing day we pressed on.

One night I got up, opened a beer and sat at my kitchen table alone. I thought to myself, "After all, I have been an undercover agent with an impressive record. I'm still young and at the top of my game. We have enough manpower, good experienced detectives and the newest equipment and technology. Still though, here we sit with nothing, not a clue or lead to go on. What have I missed? What else can we do?"

The next day we had a meeting about the progress on the case. While pacing the floor, I said to Levi, "This is just hard to believe. These guys must really be good. We've got to get something on them soon. Check for me, will you, and see if there have been any new leads at all."

He stood up, "I know, boss, its damn funny there are no other prints, no evidence, nothing. I'll check with the other detectives. They are reviewing everything and I'll report back to you tomorrow."

"Thanks, Levi, let's hope we get a break in this case soon," I said.

Chapter 39

Three months later, investigations were still going on regarding the bank robbery and we were stressed out because we had so little evidence and no suspects.

Our stress was compounded when, one morning, we received an urgent call that a jewelry store had been robbed. It was the most prestigious jeweler in town. They carried a lot of high-end merchandise and quite a lot more inventory than anyone else. The robbers evidently did their homework.

The robbery was committed in the middle of the night by people who planned every facet of the heist very carefully. The security alarm was disabled. Access was gained through a metal door with a very intricate triple lock apparatus. These doors would require talent similar to that of a safe cracker because of the strength of the metal and type of locks involved.

In a robbery like this, the insurance company detectives quickly investigate the owners. This is because of the possibility of them perhaps faking a robbery, collecting the insurance and fencing the jewelry later. That scenario was quickly ruled out, especially in light of the fact that the owners had not insured a lot of the jewelry. This was a solid company, third generation; they were very successful and evidently didn't feel they had to insure everything in the store. Upon questioning, the owners confided that they never dreamed they would be robbed.

There had to be at least three thieves. Heavy plate glass had been broken for access to two cases where some expensive gold and precious stone jewelry were displayed. These always stayed in that case and were locked at night. All diamonds were kept in a small vault which the robbers blew open with explosive. They took everything. This heist probably netted the robbers more than the bank job had yielded.

The advantage the robbers had was that nobody knew until probably four to six hours after the robbery that one had been committed. This gave the thieves ample time to leave the scene, hide their stash, and go about business as usual.

The jewelry store had just installed a surveillance camera but unfortunately, the robbers got the cartridge out of the unit and took it with them. Again, like the bank robbery, there were no fingerprints and no one saw them. We had little evidence to go on. The robbers appeared to be quite knowledgeable about the latest security innovations, such as how to get easily through the metal triple locking door and how to blow the vault without damaging anything else in the store.

Fortunately, the better jewelry was catalogued carefully because of the values involved. Fencing them anywhere locally would be nearly impossible.

An all points bulletin including the list of stolen jewelry was sent out to all other law enforcement agents in the country. We asked them to be on the lookout, in case they stopped someone and found this type of jewelry. Our U.S. contacts were notified as well.

In our investigation of this heist, I consulted a man who had been a successful jewelry fencer. He assisted me in identifying the top jewelry-fencing people in the whole north of Mexico and southern U.S. Two years prior, we had arrested him and I felt it would be useful to have a specialist to consult. Because he hadn't actually committed a robbery, I recommended to the magistrate that he not be prosecuted, but that he must help us whenever we needed his expertise and knowledge.

The fence, a jovial round faced, heavy set man with a straggly moustache, had never fenced anything remotely as valuable as the loot from this robbery. He told us that what he had fenced in the past had been cat burglar type of small things, a few at a time, but that he had never been involved in any big money merchandise. "It was just a sideline to earn a little extra money," he told me with a wink.

The names of well-known jewelry fencers that he gave us were distributed to the law enforcement agencies throughout the region and they were to be very discreet about the names involved.

We speculated whether these robbers had come in from out of town and the mastermind decided Mexicali might be a good place to perform these robberies. We didn't know for sure. We felt that our police force was as good as any other towns'. In fact, nightly routine checks of businesses were done more often than elsewhere.

I thought the fact that there was only one door in the jewelry store was unusual. The owner had installed iron bars on the windows and a triple lock door. I decided to check with the fire chief about this. I asked him, "How, in the world would someone survive a fire in that building. How would you rescue someone in this store if a fire broke out?"

The fire chief reported that they had not seen the iron bars on the windows and that they may have been added since the last inspection. When we checked with the owners, they said, yes, they had installed them when they did a remodel on the offices and never thought to check with anyone about it. The owner said they hadn't even thought of fire. There were no electrical appliances whatsoever in the store and the electrical system was nearly brand new. Little did I know that the installation of barred windows would eventually affect our case.

Chapter 40

Before we completed the investigation of the jewelry heist, another robbery took place. It was at a large manufacturing company, very early on a Friday morning before the business opened. Because it paid employees in cash, the company received a large amount of currency from its bank late the evening before to dole out payroll. It was not unusual back then for companies to pay their employees in cash. Once a month, each employee received a manila business size envelope, which contained his or her pay slip and cash. The envelope was sealed and the employee's name typed on a label. The thieves had to have known about this.

The bank robbery hadn't required an explosive specialist. It was carried out in slick fashion in that those talents weren't necessary. Again access was gained through a very thick metal door with the same kind of triple lock as the jewelry store. The safe had also to be cracked in order for them to get at the cash.

The cash that was ready for this payroll was unmarked. None would be traceable and the robbers took everything in the safe including about $10,000 more than the payroll itself which was in the neighborhood of $60,000.

These robbers were very shrewd. Once again we were unable to obtain any leads. There were no fingerprints, and no one saw or heard anything during or after the robberies. We were all extremely frustrated. We desperately wanted to catch these criminals and get them behind bars.

Word was received from higher up that we were to put extra men on this case and to do everything in our power to solve these crimes as soon as possible.

What a terrible time it was for me, and, of course, for the entire police force. Everyone had worked extra hours and given their best. After all, this was what we did, it was who we were; we caught criminals. Yes, we were hell bent on capturing these damn robbers. Our emotions running up and down like a roller coaster, we had trouble sleeping, were nervous and short tempered and our usual good humor was gone.

Since I was Chief of Police, I felt heat more than the other officers. I was called in to meet with my superiors and asked what is the problem with catching these crooks. How demeaning those meetings were. My answers were honest though.

Reporting regularly to them, I explained that we had done everything possible; worked everyone overtime, pored over every facet of the case, reexamined every single detail we had on the robberies. I asked if I could bring on board two crime investigators from Mexico City who specialized in high tech robberies. Permission was granted for the hiring the two for consultation purposes.

By this time, I just wanted the cases solved any way we could get it done because the longer this went on, the worse it looked for me. My reputation was excellent until this fiasco.

We kept trying to come up with some answers. The two specialists from Mexico City were working well with us, but we still had nothing. I did ask if we could offer rewards and was told that the request would be submitted and an answer would be forthcoming.

The press was brutal, keeping the stories in the news constantly with lines like: "Police have apprehended no suspects in the three crime spree robberies." Or: "What is holding up justice?" and "Law enforcement officers in Mexicali unable to solve triple crime spree!" There were many,

many more unfortunate headlines and stories. Radio broadcasts followed suit.

The community buzzed with the failure of our department to capture any rogues for these robberies. It was the favorite topic of conversation from the baby carriage pushing moms in the park to the old men in the taverns. Everyone just had to keep talking about it. When I stopped for coffee at my favorite café on my way to work, I was barraged by questions about the robberies; what leads did we have, were we going to make any arrests soon, and on and on. My good humor was wearing very thin.

Authorization came down from headquarters two days later that a reward was to be offered to anyone who could give us solid leads on any of these three robberies. Reward notices were published in all the newspapers. But still no one came forward. A very long week went by. Progress is so slow, I said to myself. Are these damn cases ever going to get solved? My superior had sent the specialists back to Mexico City since they hadn't been able to crack the case either.

One Saturday found Levi and me sitting in the back corner of the tavern, downing our beers, trying to relax a little.

Conversation drifted to the robberies before long though and we were at it again. "Surely someone will come forward," Levi said. "The reward should flush them out."

"Man, let them come on in, we need a break real bad." I responded. We ordered another beer and vowed not to ruin our whole day talking about the robbery. Instead we made plans to take a trip to the hills and go do some target practice. This was the first weekend we had taken off in two months. Everyone was so bushed; I thought it best for us all to get away for that weekend and come back refreshed on Monday. The jailers and regular law enforcement officers worked, but the rest of us who had been doing the investigating were off.

The next week, after the reward notice was published in the paper, we got a call from a man saying he must speak to us but in total confidence. He asked that we meet him in a museum across town the next morning. He refused to come to the police station, because he thought someone would see him and was frightened. Assurance was given him and we arranged the meeting.

Levi and I met him at the designated time at the museum and were able to sit in a lounge. It was early enough that no other patrons had arrived. The slender, middle-aged man showed up on time and was very nervous and scared. He wore work clothes: a worn denim long-sleeved shirt open at the neck and faded jeans with scruffy edges where they skimmed the toes of cowboy boots that had seen better days. As he sat forward in his chair, he again asked us if this would be kept totally confidential. We assured him it would.

He related that his girl friend was working at a popular bar on the other side of town and shared with him a conversation she had overheard one night after work. She served margaritas and appetizers to a table of four men. Over the course of a long evening, they drank several rounds and she had joked with them and they had teased her. She had even asked if they worked nearby. One man said, yes, that he owned a taxicab company in the city. He named the cab company and she didn't think much about it. The others were in conversation and didn't reply. But later, she delivered another round to them in the crowded bar, and upon nearing their table, overheard one man say, no, that loot is going to be hidden for a long time, it would be insane to move it now. You shut up about it. I don't want to hear anymore! That was all she heard because they stopped talking as she neared their table.

We asked if she would be willing to talk to us and he said yes, that she had been planning to call about this. I gave him my card and told him to have her call at the earliest opportunity.

Rosa called that very afternoon. After being reassured that she would get a reward if her information was useful to us, she agreed to a meeting. We met her in a park near her apartment. Trees and abundant plants and flowers lent privacy. She was nervous but told us the name of the cab company and gave us good descriptions of the men.

Now we knew we were looking for two men; a tall, middle aged man with long hair pulled back in a pony tail. He wore glasses. The second fellow was younger, short and heavy set. He had dressed in slacks and a dress shirt. Gold chains hung from his neck and from one dangled a large gold cross. On his left hand was a wide gold wedding band.

Rosa remembered their first names. We again thanked her, assuring her that the information would be kept strictly confidential.

Excitement at finally getting a breakthrough in the case was felt by our whole department.

Until Rosa and her boy friend came forward, frustration at the slow progress of the investigation had really worn me down. Now I couldn't wait to run with it.

Of course our first background check was on the cab company owner. He had given her his correct name, Javier, but he had no record at all. There was nothing we could do, but pick him up and bring him in for questioning.

We told him that his cab had been seen at the scene of two robberies. We were trying to see if he'd cave and if he was involved in the other robberies. He was advised that witnesses saw him at the scene and described him and the cab perfectly.

Javier was cool and calm, insisting that it must have been a coincidence that his cab was near where the robberies took place. Levi left the room for coffee and I spent that time telling our cabby that I would personally make sure things went easy for him. I reminded him that in my position of police chief, I had the authority to make it happen. He didn't budge.

Levi returned with coffee and donuts. After I grabbed a donut, I scooted my chair back, walked to the door, looked back and said, "Have to go; the boss is waiting for a progress report on this case and he wants it right now."

As I watched and listened through the two way mirror, Levi started putting the pressure on. He stood up, shaking his fist repeatedly at Javier and growling, "Do you have any damn idea how bad things will go for you if you don't cooperate soon? If you wait until the Chief loses his temper, you will be making a bad mistake. He'll lock you up and throw away the key!"

It took hours of interrogation for us to break him down. We told him if he wanted to drag this out, he wouldn't see his family for a long time. He winced but still wouldn't talk. We both left the room and let him think on that for a time. After returning, we applied more pressure, both by threatening Javier with hard time in the worst prison in North Mexico and by informing him that we were going to bring his wife in to witness the interrogation. Levi and I left again, had a sandwich and rested some, occasionally watching our suspect through the double glass. Javier was given only water but no food during this time.

He was now pacing, frowning and holding the back of his hand to his forehead. After about an hour we began working again to unlock Javier. I told him to sit down and listen closely, then I pointed out that when the robbers found out that we had picked him up already, (and they would find out because the cab wasn't running,) they may quickly kidnap his wife and children in hopes of securing his silence. Levi then waited about 15 minutes and said," Javier, do you really think they won't go after your family? These guys are pros and have a lot to lose. Your only hope is to cooperate with us and your family will immediately be protected."

I chimed in, "How do you think your wife and kids are going to manage if you are jailed for a long time? Have you thought of that? You better take this chance to tell us what we need to know or the offer of a light sentence, protection for your family and keeping your cab is off the table." Standing up, walking right up to Javier, I took hold of his shoulder and shook him, "It's now or never buddy; what'll it be?"

He actually got tears in his eyes and was shaking as he told us that he had never been in trouble in his life but needed money very badly for his family. Their youngest son was ill and needed ongoing medical care. The cab company wasn't doing that well, too much competition, and he had met a man and become friends with him and was talked in to driving getaway for the three jobs.

Javier hung his head as he told us that he had come from a good family and knew he was doing wrong. He had felt so desperate that he went along with the job. "I have never ever been in trouble before in my life!" he lamented. He then gave us the names and addresses of the robbers.

We had promised him that if he gave up the others, things would go lightly for him. Obviously he had to be charged and given a sentence or the others would know he had given them up, but once his sentence had begun, he could be transferred to another jail and then released.

Now, with the names and addresses of the three robbers, we were able to begin constant surveillance. Bugs were placed in their homes, and on their phones. Homing devices were hidden on their cars. They were leading surprisingly normal lives. One of the perpetrators worked as a chef at a local restaurant, the other installed security windows and equipment. That was a great way to case a business and he, no doubt, had targeted the jewelry store after installing the bars on the windows there. Both men were single and shared an apartment. Their new girlfriends had been high priced call girls. The girls were sporting some fine diamond and gold jewelry too. At the best night spots, the robbers were seen with their girlfriends.

The third member of the gang was in the import-export business. Married with five young children, his family had recently moved into a new home in the suburbs. Rosa had described him: the younger, shorter one wearing the gold jewelry.

After three weeks, we had all the evidence needed and made our plans for finally picking up the thieves, who had been, without a doubt, true professionals.

Three squad cars and three back up cars, all with sharp shooters, were assembled. The robbers each had to be picked up fast so they couldn't tip the others off by phone or any other way. The arrests were made at night and went very smoothly. First we picked up the two that lived in the same apartment. They were drinking beer and watching TV when we arrived. We then picked up the other who was alone at his new home. His wife had taken the children to visit her mother, like she did every Thursday night.

The men had no idea they had been found out. They were not armed and were smart enough to cooperate peacefully. They insisted they didn't understand why they were being arrested. We read them their rights but gave them no other information about why they were being arrested until they were in the interrogation room. At that time, they were each booked separately and charged with the robberies. They were kept apart, in separate interrogation rooms. This way, we could tell them the others had cracked and admitted the entire stories of the robberies pinning everything on the man we were talking to. Our crooks were intelligent and they knew we had all three of them in custody. We hadn't been questioning them long when each quietly told us that they didn't wish to discuss it further. They each asked that their attorney be present. Attorneys were contacted and represented the robbers. Justice was done though, the judge convicted them and sent them to prison for a minimum of 30 years.

The jewelry was all found and confiscated at the home of the two single men. It had been locked in fireproof metal boxes and placed under the bed. Blankets had been wrapped around each box to hide it. They weren't very big boxes, but the jewelry contained in them was some of the finest and most expensive. The owners of the jewelry store couldn't thank us enough. About three fourths of the money from the payroll heist was recovered and the bank money that had been placed in the safety deposit boxes was returned. The cash the robbers took had already been spent.

It was a great relief to have them behind bars, although we were really disappointed that they were caught because of the reward offer and not entirely because of our good investigative efforts. Never in my military career or when I was Chief of Police had I ever seen cases that lacked any evidence with which to investigate. Always we could glean at least some bits of evidence about a crime, however scant.

This case would probably have been cracked when the thieves eventually tried to fence the jewelry which was well described to all the dealers we could locate in Mexico and the U.S. It took almost five months to break the case.

Many other investigations needed attention, so the department moved on to other crimes, and yet we never forgot the humbling days and weeks spent on those robberies. Levi and I talked of them from time to time over a beer in the evening after a hard day's work and lamented our frustrations.

Chapter 41

One uneventful day about eight months after my time with Yadira, a young woman walked shyly into the police station. The blind on the big window between my office and the reception area was open, and I watched her enter. I could hear her when she said, "I'm Isabel Enriquez, and I've come to apply for the job advertised in the paper." The deputy at the front desk buzzed me and said, "Can I send her in?"

I replied, "Yes, send the young lady in." I stood up, walked over to her, and introduced myself. I motioned to a chair for her to sit in. Behind the desk, across from her, I leaned back in my chair and said, "Glad to meet you. We've had the ad in the paper for a week and quite a few applicants have dropped off their resumes and filled out applications. I've looked them over but haven't called anyone in for interviews because none of them really had enough experience."

"Your ad said you wanted only experienced applicants," she answered. "I worked as a secretary for the Monterrey Police Department for three years. My boss gave me this recommendation when I moved back here." She leaned forward and handed me the letter.

She wore just a hint of fragrance, light and delicate like roses. I couldn't help noticing her youthful figure and quick smile. Her long black hair was pulled straight back, fastened, and then fell halfway down her back. Tight fitting jeans, a western shirt, denim vest and western boots made up her attire and she looked sensational. I had to refocus quickly and told her, "The position is still open and we need someone as soon as possible."

As I took the recommendation letter from her hand, I could hardly stop looking into her eyes. I recovered my senses and asked, "You said you moved back here; is this your home town?"

"Yes, it is. I moved to Monterrey where my sister and her husband live. I was able to stay with them while I took a law and justice course at the college. A job was available in the police department there so I tried for it and got it. It was a good job and I liked it, but our parents live here and my father had a stroke. He is better, but they need me. I find I am enjoying being home with my family and friends."

"Well, Miss. Enriquez," I said, as I read over the paperwork, "Your recommendation is certainly good. You evidently have the type of experience we need." I told her the wage we were offering and she said, "Thank you. That is acceptable to me."

"We have to run a background check on you, but it only takes a couple days. How soon can you start work?"

"Well, today is Tuesday; do you think next Monday is alright?"

"Yes, that works well for us. Let me show you around and then we can come back to my office and discuss your schedule. I can answer any questions you may have about the job."

After introducing her to the three officers on duty, I led Isabel to what would be her office and with a welcoming sweep of my hand said, "What do you think?"

"I like this because it has nice windows. I didn't have a window in my last office. I feel comfortable with the staff too, they all seem friendly."

"They are all good people, I assure you. I'm glad you'll be working with us."

"Monday, take some time to get settled in and let me know if there is anything you need. Deputy John will show you the supply room, how we log things as we use them and instruct you on use of the police radios. Even though there is a dispatch officer on duty all the time, everyone has to be proficient on the radios. You will have time to get comfortable with all of this."

I walked her leisurely back to my office. She said she didn't have any questions so I led her out of the building onto the porch. "You'll do fine, Isabel. I'll see you Monday about eight."

She smiled as she turned to leave, "I'm looking forward to it."

Our jail was fairly typical, a bit stark but at least it was a fairly new building with more amenities than some of the older jails. In the very front of the building was a waiting area which had several hard back chairs, a couple end tables and a coffee table with the usual magazines. Wanted posters were displayed on a large cork board on one wall. Opposite that area were offices which were entered through doors off the center hall. First was Deputy John's office, next a radio dispatcher and an officer shared, then Isabel's office. All had a window facing toward the waiting area and a window on the outside wall giving them a view of a small, fenced courtyard. The courtyard was private with benches and a few flowers blooming where we could take our breaks.

My office was larger and spanned most of the back of the building. The jail was on the second floor.

The rest of the week seemed to go by slowly and finally it was Monday. As I got ready for work, I thought happily, "It's the day Isabel begins work."

She was a few minutes early, looking pretty, and seemed enthusiastic about her new job. I met her in the hall and offered her coffee. After pouring us each a cup, we went to my office. Isabel sipped her coffee, "This smells good and it's nice and hot." I asked her if she had any questions and she said no. After we had our coffee I said, "We'll go out front and you can settle in to your office." As we walked down the hall, I told her, "Don't hesitate to call on any of the officers or me if you have questions or need anything."

She thanked me and went about organizing her space. When I returned to my office I realized that there was the lingering fragrance of her. How pleasant, but I had to tackle the work stacked up on my desk.

Chapter 42

In the days that followed, it was apparent that Isabel was quick, efficient and an asset to us right away, not to mention the fact that she brightened the place considerably.

The next week, Isabel's mom and dad came by the station as she was getting off work. They were going to take her to dinner. She introduced us and I liked them at once. Her father, John, was a tall man, still quite handsome, with graying hair and moustache. He smiled a lot and held the hand of his wife for support. Carole was medium height, her hair was still dark and the gaze from her eyes was direct. When she smiled, it transformed her from pretty to beautiful. It was easy to see where Isabel got her looks. John and I started talking about the local news and then he said, "Manuel, why don't you join us, we're just going to the little café down the street."

"That sounds good to me, I just need a minute to lock up and I'll meet you there." I replied.

After washing up quickly, I put on a clean, pressed shirt that I had hanging in the closet in my office and headed to the cafe. I joined them at their table. We had a beer and enjoyed conversation and dinner. They told me to stop by their home anytime. I thanked them and told them I would.

Work was busy and I went on a couple out of town trips to San Diego for meetings. Isabel settled in to her job. One morning after she had been there about a month and a half, she asked if I would like to stop by their home and meet her grandma who lived right next door to Isabel's family. Grandma Rose had heard a lot about the police station from Isabel and since she didn't get around very well, Isabel thought she would enjoy meeting me and hearing a little about police business. Evidently Grandma loved mysteries and hearing about real crime. Seeing Isabel was enticing enough, although I was glad to meet Grandma. We agreed that Saturday morning would be a good time for my visit.

When I pulled in and parked my car, I briefly greeted her folks, then Isabel took me next door and into the back yard where Rose was sitting. She was perky with a quick smile, a small woman, wearing a faded yellow dress. Despite the warmth of the day, she had worn a light sweater over her shoulders. Her hair was white and she wore it long with barrettes on either side of her head to hold it out of her eyes. Her skin was dark and wrinkled, showing she had spent a lot of time outdoors.

She said, "Welcome, have a chair. "Isabel, will you get us sodas?"

"Of Course," Isabel replied and left for the kitchen.

The chairs were from an old metal dinette set, a bit bent, but served as lawn chairs on the patio. I told Rose about a few of the cases that had been recently solved and she asked questions about how we worked through the evidence. She leaned forward with interest, bright eyed, enjoying hearing about real cases and asked lots of questions which I answered. What a sharp mind she had, I thought at the time.

The sun was warm and I felt relaxed there in Rose's back yard. After we finished our sodas and bid her good bye, Isabel walked me back to my car. I said, "Isabel, why don't you join me for lunch? I'm starved and don't want to eat alone. I'll drive you home later."

She said with no hesitation, "Well, alright" and told her parents she'd be gone awhile.

I drove to a cozy café nearby. Isabel was relaxed and we talked and laughed on the way. We sat in a private little booth in the back. When the waiter came to take our order, I said, "Isabel, let's have a margarita before we order lunch."

Leaning forward and meeting my gaze, she said, "Sounds good."

"Bring us two," I told the waiter.

"Right away sir," he replied.

When the waiter returned with the drinks, we were talking softly. I told Isabel how much I enjoyed her company, and asked her if she knew how beautiful she was. I don't even remember reaching for her hand, but I was holding it.

She said, "Manuel, I have been thinking about you a lot and find you quite attractive. I must confess that I asked Deputy John if you were single and he raised his eyebrows, grinned and said, 'Yes.' "

"He told you right, honey," I replied just as the waiter returned to take our order.

Over lunch, we talked, flirted and laughed. When I dropped her at her home, she leaned over and gave me a kiss that left me breathless. She waved goodbye as she entered the house. I sped off feeling elated about our time together.

This was our first date, but by no means our last. After that we saw each other every spare minute that we weren't at work. We laughed and shared our hopes and dreams. I could relax when I was with her. When I acted too macho, she chided me lovingly. That didn't set well with me at first, but she was probably right as that machismo, while normal for we Mexican males, wasn't appreciated by our women. I was no longer in such a hurry in my conquest of a woman at this time of my life. I had learned to take my time.

Thinking what a welcome addition Isabel was to my life, I realized that I hadn't admitted to myself how lonely I was. The few women I had dated in recent months were attractive but there just wasn't any spark or magic between them and me.

Thoughts of mysterious Yadira had come and gone. We may have been able to make it if she could have moved past her problems, if she had been willing to start over with me, but that was not the case.

Chapter 43

I was puzzled thinking about the women I had loved. For various reasons things hadn't worked out with any of them. Soul searching and thinking about how I treated them occupied my mind. What could I have done different? The answers came to me slowly and Isabel helped me discover them.

Isabel was intelligent, lively and fun to be with. She was 25 at the time and I was 37. Hard work did not seem to bother her. She was honest and forthright in her relationship with me. If she didn't like something, she told me. If I asked her to go somewhere and it didn't suit her, she would let me know. I like that kind of honesty. When I'm someplace with a woman and she acts like she is not having any fun, neither of us has a good time.

One Sunday, Isabel packed a picnic and we drove out of town where it was quiet and serene and enjoyed the day. She relaxed with a good book and I sketched scenery to paint later. It was a warm sunny day that I remember well. Birds were singing and darting in and out of the big cacti. There were yellow and red blooms on a couple varieties of cactus and butterflies and bees were taking advantage of the open flowers.

One evening, we went out for a drink, then a few appetizers. A good band was playing so we danced. It was a delightful evening and as soon as we were in the car, I asked her to come to my home for a nightcap. She agreed.

We were sitting on the couch having a glass of wine when she put hers down, looked at me and leaned over close. My wine glass missed the table as I set it down and broke, spilling on the floor. "Don't worry about it," I murmured, as I met her lips with mine. We held each other tightly kissing. I stopped, breathless, and told her I loved her. She murmured that she loved me, too. Isabel stayed the night and it was perfect. She was not shy and we made love until dawn.

Looking back, I remember that night; the moment when my wine glass fell, broke, and spilled on the floor as Isabel leaned to kiss me.

I loved her madly and thought about her every waking moment. Even though she was eleven years younger than me, this didn't seem to pose any problem for either one of us, although I secretly wondered if I should be worried about our age difference. What if she wanted a younger man in a few years? Would she get bored with me?

Isabel shared her concerns regarding my prior marriages and children. She was still young and wanted a family. She asked detailed questions about the reasons for my failed marriages. I answered her as honestly as I could. My youth no doubt had a lot to do with the first two disastrous marriages. I was immature and didn't have any idea what was involved with being a husband and supporting a wife. My military service also took a toll with Marlena and me. Military assignments just kept me gone too much to give her the attention that a young wife needs. Frequent absences also hampered being the kind of father that I wanted to be.

My previous wives were also young when we married so they didn't even know their minds. The crushing responsibilities of marriage and motherhood were a quick reality and they were as unprepared as I. Now I knew what those responsibilities entailed.

I asked Isabel to marry me after we had been going together for about eight months. She accepted with a warm hug. We began planning our wedding.

Chapter 44

Because of department policy, we could not both work at the police department once we were married, Isabel and I discussed this and she told me she had heard about an opening in an attorney's office nearby. I suggested she try for it and that we would wait to announce our engagement until she found employment elsewhere. We both thought it would be a mistake to work together anyway. Isabel applied for the legal position and was hired right away.

In my excitement over our wedding, I decided to parachute out of a plane and land right in the Plaza just before the ceremony. It seemed a daring idea, probably, because I wanted to show off at the time. The jump would have placed me right in front of the big church there where I thought we could get married.

This idea was a little complicated and Isabel was not in favor of it. She thought it dangerous and unconventional. Weddings are all about the bride and I wanted Isabel to be happy more than anything. Upon further reflection, the parachute landing was canceled. Instead we had a small wedding service at a smaller church with our close friends and family.

In spite of it being modest, our wedding day was special. My bride wore her mother's antique dress with the lace scarf typical of that era for the veil. Her hair flowed down her back luxuriously under the veil. She looked radiant. I rented a Mexican dress suit, the type with tight pants and short bolero jacket. Since Isabel was wearing a vintage dress, a modern tuxedo wouldn't have gone very well with it. Isabel appreciated the suit that complimented her ensemble. I wore a sombrero too. Isabel's sister was her maid of honor and wore a red dress. My best man, Carlos wore a grey western cut suit. Flowers for the wedding were red and of several varieties. The bright colored flowers with multicolored ribbons in the church and reception hall added to the festive mood. Our wedding cake was the usual tropical fruitcake filled with pineapple chunks, grated coconut and sliced pecans decorated with coconut flavored white frosting.

Everything went smoothly. After we left the church, we went to a hall we had rented. There were typical Mexican foods including spicy rice, beans, and tortilla dishes with chicken and barbecued beef. Sangria and beer were offered as well as soft drinks and coffee.

Our friends had arranged for a mariachi band as their gift to us. The band was dressed in white tight fitting trousers, white boots and red shirts with matching boleros. A money dance was started by my best man. Friends and relatives take turns dancing with the bride and groom and put a donation in a box decorated for this purpose. They then presented the box to us. What a time we had; children, parents and people of all ages dancing and singing. Everyone was happy for us and joined the fun.

After an appropriate time, when the party started to wind down a little, we slipped away. I had made a reservation that night for us to stay in the honeymoon suite at a nearby hotel. Isabel was pleased when she saw the lovely rooms. Our first night as husband and wife was not disappointing. In each others' arms we shared love, passion, and excitement until late that night.

We left the next day for our honeymoon. We took a week off work and went by car to the beach on the Baja Peninsula.

Baja California's highway curves and switches up and over the sierras, drops down to the Sea of Cortez and is interesting because of the many different types of scenery. The road follows the coast with sheer cliffs dropping down to clear, blue water. Clouds partly shroud volcanic peaks in the distance. Boats dot the blue water of the sea. Everything seemed magical

We drove only to Enemata and then Colonet, a few hours from Mexicali. We wanted to relax and enjoy our honeymoon, not spend so much time on the road. Our first two nights were spent on the water's edge at an out of the way motel at Ensenada. It was quiet and peaceful, with plenty of privacy. We spent many hours lounging in bed. After all we were just married and I wasn't going to disappoint my bride. Not only was the sex great, but we formed a bond between of us closeness, loving and caring. Isabel whispered in my ear late one night, "We are really good together!" I murmured, "You are so right." Our room was upstairs overlooking the ocean and French doors led out to a balcony. Comfortable lounge chairs and a little table made it a perfect choice for our morning coffee and enjoying breathtaking sunsets at night.

Next we drove south and had reservations at a secluded resort in Colonet. Lodging here was in small bungalows called "casitas." These were separate from the other units and right on the beach. We could hear the waves as we lay lazily in our bed.

When we did dress and exit our casita to eat, we were able to dine right at the resort. Food was prepared in an open-air kitchen. Local fishermen provided fresh lobster daily and we ordered it most evenings. Locally grown fruits and vegetables and home baked goods were offered and all delicious. We spent five nights relaxing. We enjoyed walks on the beach, basking in the sun and watching the whales. Our goal was to slow down. After all, honeymooning must be relaxing, unhurried and romantic.

One evening, because the proprietor knew we were on our honeymoon, he arranged to have the mariachi band playing that night come by our table and serenade us. Isabel loved that. We danced into the night as the music became slow and romantic. I whispered to her, "I will love you forever and never forget this moment."

She sighed, looked right into my eyes and pressed her body closer to mine. In my heart I knew Isabel loved me as much as I loved her.

Happy and rested, we returned to Mexicali to begin married life.

Chapter 45

I vowed to make this marriage work. My job was demanding, but I was determined to keep Isabel well informed of what was going on and be thoughtful about any time I would have to be late returning home. My prior marriages were shattered by my being away from home too much. I had been inconsiderate of my past wives' feelings and needs. I didn't want to make the same mistake again with Isabel.

I informed my boss that whenever possible, I wished to have my wife accompany me to our regular out-of-town meetings. He agreed as his own marriage had been a long and happy one. In fact, I sought his advice from time to time.

Isabel was a good, loving wife and kept our house clean. She was an excellent cook and our nights were filled with love and deep caring. She was a sexy woman and we enjoyed a passionate, vigorous sex life. Her willingness to experiment and the fact that she seemed to enjoy it as much as I did made ours a happy marriage.

Isabel had mentioned a few times in the first year of our marriage that she didn't like the risks involved in my position as Police Chief of Mexicali. She wanted to start our family and was concerned about the danger I sometimes faced. Patiently I reminded her that I was very well trained for this type of work. I promised to be careful and not to take unnecessary chances in the line of duty. She surprised me, though, with her ever increasing demand that we should quit our jobs and move to L.A. where her sister lived.

I thought about how important my job was to me. I loved my work. The salary was good, and I had gotten regular wage increases. Another of my big reasons for resisting a move was the distance it would put between my two boys and me. I wondered maybe since Isabel had not yet become a parent, she couldn't fully understand my concerns. I decided to change the subject and hoped after thinking about it, Isabel may change her mind.

Chapter 46

In the second year of our marriage Isabel announced that she was pregnant. We were happy about the baby. We decided that she should quit her job and take care of herself during the pregnancy and then, of course, stay home with the baby. She soon gave notice, quit her job, and seemed happy about starting our family. However, after a short time at home, Isabel became insistent and told me again, "I want you to quit your job." She wanted us to move to Los Angeles. "Our baby would be born in the U.S. and be an American citizen. Opportunities would be available in the U.S. for our child. Citizenship is getting more difficult to obtain for Hispanics. Manuel, you know that."

I tried to explain to her once again that I loved my job, was due for a salary increase and was uncertain about job prospects across the border. Quite frankly, I wasn't all that fond of L.A.

I argued that she should be close to her mother when the baby was born. She persisted. I told her that it would be all the more difficult to see my boys in Mexico

City if we moved any further away. "Maybe since you aren't a parent yet, you can't fully understand my concerns about moving yet further from my boys."

At that point we were at a standoff. Both of us were too mad to talk anymore. We began to argue regularly. I stalled for time, but she never let up at all. One day, when she was about six months along, I came home in the evening and found that she had packed a bag. It was sitting by the door. She met me in the hall. My heart was pounding. "I'm taking the bus to L.A. tomorrow. This baby is going to be born in America. I wish you would have listened and made arrangements to come with me."

"Oh Isabel, I can't walk out on my job without notice." She stared coldly and didn't answer. "Fine, I said. "Since you are hell bent to go, I'll give notice, sell the house and join you in L.A. What kind of a job do you think I'll get? Have you thought of that?"

She stood looking at me sternly, hands on her hips and answered: "I have thought about your work. Manuel, you know how to do police work, mechanic work and you can learn any trade fast. My brother in law is an iron worker for a heavy construction company. He told me he might be able to get you on with the company he works for. It's a good paying job."

I couldn't even answer her. I felt she was not the least concerned whether I would be happy in the U.S. or not. After a time, I looked back at her and said, "I'm sorry. I need time to think about all of this. Can't you wait a little longer?"

"No, you know how I feel about this." She took a step toward me and put her hand on my shoulder. "Please understand how badly I want to move." She truly looked on America as the land of milk and honey. She figured endless opportunities awaited us.

"Alright," I said. "I'll take you to the bus tomorrow and see what I can work out here. You've backed me right into a corner, Isabel." I turned away from her. "You know you are everything to me. I would never even consider this move for any other woman. I turned back, taking a deep breath. "Only for you, Isabel. You knew I would because you know how I feel about you."

My anger was hard to hide. I was also suffering hurt pride. The man in the household usually has the say. I'm sure Isabel knew I was upset. The problem was she didn't seem to be worried about my concerns at all. I said very little to her and gave her a quick kiss goodbye when I took her to the bus the next day. She asked when we parted: "Are you going to join me soon?"

"You know I love you. I need to think about all this. Call me as soon as you arrive at your sister's house."

I was still cool and half angry when she called to tell me she had arrived safely. I felt she was manipulating me big time.

After Isabel left, though, I quickly began to miss her and worried about her having the baby without me. I loved her madly and knew I had to be with her. By the time two weeks went by, I was suffering.

I decided to write Isabel. However, my mind could only grasp parts of sentences, maybe half sentences mulling around in my brain. Finally, I decided I must just do it, write her and tell her how I really felt. I was still having trouble concentrating, but when I took pencil and paper in hand, calmness returned to me and I was able to begin.

Isabel, I couldn't imagine living without you, you have made a great change in my life. It is incredible that me, seated in a chair, can write everything I think and can't say to you right now. They tell me that in this last two years, I was laughing a lot. I've always been a rude type and a lot of my feelings were not very open but what changes!

Isabel, you have made so much difference in the way I think and many changes in the way I feel. I also recognize that this facet of my personality has made me so much more agreeable and you have made me know this.

Isabel, I have desires to be able to shout that I love you and be able to do it so forcefully that you could hear me. You find me as you find me and as such, you enter my world one more time. Note that I, Manuel Velasquez, love you, like surely no one else has on this planet named earth. I couldn't have known that you would find out or much less that you would have known that I loved you so much. I don't want to relinquish or distract my mind. Precisely my punishment is that I can't stop thinking about you.

THAT UNTIL THE FINAL MOMENT OF MY EXISTENCE YOUR NAME WILL ALWAYS BE SPOKEN BY THESE LIPS THAT HAVE KISSED YOU. AFTER THIS

MOMENT WHEN THE KARMA LETS YOU FEEL AND PERHAPS TAKES AWAY FROM ME THE GIFT OF SPEECH, I WILL THINK OF YOU ALWAYS UNTIL THE LAST MOMENT, UNTIL THE TIMES CROSS, UNTIL WHERE FEAR IS GONE OF BEING ALONE BEFORE THE LACK OF LIGHT.

Today is 9:25 P.M. on Saturday, and I am dying, Isabel, to see you. How can I bear it? I don't know, I can no longer write. I desire with all my heart that we be together, that you love me even though it was a LITTLE BIT. Do You Suffer? Like me? I think not.

After addressing an envelope and affixing a stamp, I put my pen down. Though I had written from my heart, was it going to be enough to make Isabel understand? The next morning I woke up early. Most of the night I couldn't sleep and tossed and turned. Would Isabel get the letter and call me? Was I doing the right thing quitting my job and moving? What choice did I have? I had a new baby on the way and a wife I dearly loved. Of course I had to go, they needed me.

Obviously, I was in quite a state at the time I wrote the letter. The next three days were terrible. In fact I did something I never did. I called my superior and told him I needed the day off. I had a splitting headache and tried to rest some and wondered if Isabel got my letter and what she would think.

When Isabel received my letter, she called me immediately and assured me of her feelings and that the difference in our ages was never a problem. She asked if I would make the proper arrangements and come to her. "I am also suffering terribly without you." she said.

I replied, "Yes, my darling, I'll hasten everything along and join you soon."

"I will count the hours." Isabel answered.

The next day I gave my two week notice to my boss but also told him I needed the following Friday off to make a two night trip to L.A. He said, no problem, and wished me luck. After all, he knew about women and love.

Then I put the house up for sale and left for L.A.

It was dark when I finally got there and I was tired, but so anxious to see my wife. While driving I thought about what the future might bring. I was old enough and had been through enough in my 36 years to know that one really never knows what may lie ahead. Isabel heard my pickup and met me before I even walked to the house. We held each other close and I was kissing her and kissing her hair, which always smelled so good. She clung to me and said, "I'm so glad you are here! The next day when we had some privacy and got the chance to talk face to face, Isabel apologized for being so adamant about us moving, but she said she still thought it best. She asked me to please understand how badly she wanted to move to the U.S. She said our child would have so many more opportunities and she felt we would as well. I couldn't argue that she, at least, would probably have more opportunities than women in Mexico.

Chapter 47

My brother-in-law took me to meet his boss at the construction company late Friday afternoon. The boss was a pleasant man, yet all business. He told me about the skyscraper they were building. We talked about the job and he asked some questions about my experiences, prior work, military career (I could not divulge much of it) and family situation. I didn't share with the boss that I had been ; I just told him I had been a cop so he wouldn't think me over qualified. He then offered me a job on the spot.

I was to join the union as an apprentice ironworker and work up to journeyman. He said he thought I was bright and hard working so could reach journeyman status within one year. I agreed to the terms and was to report for work two Mondays later.

I couldn't help wondering what this job would be like, so completely different than anything I had ever done. Confusion and worry plagued me about the move. Isabel had thrown me some curves, had known my feelings about moving and persisted. I couldn't apply for work in law enforcement in L.A. I hadn't been in the country long enough, the legal process was vastly different from Mexico and all I had was a green card, not citizenship.

I had to send money to my boys and because of the new baby Isabel wouldn't be working soon. Of course, we would have another mouth to feed.

Upon my return to Mexicali, a family who wanted to buy my house contacted me. They made an offer that was a little less than I was asking. I decided to take it. I realized a nice profit on the house and knew we would need the money for a place in L.A. I wanted Isabel and me to be settled in a home of our own as soon as possible because we needed our privacy. Our baby was due in just two months.

I had thought about things a lot in the last week in Mexicali and decided I better go to L.A. and try and make the best of it. I missed Isabel and wanted to be with her. Goodbyes were shared with friends, fellow workers and family and I headed for California.

We stayed with Isabel's sister, Carmelita, and husband Ignacio for two weeks until we found a place. They were very gracious and Ignacio told me a lot about the job and made me feel more confident about it.

Isabel and her sister looked at homes for sale during the day. At night and on the weekend, Isabel and I would look at their favorites. We decided on a nice little house in Pomona, an East Los Angeles neighborhood fairly close to Isabel's sister and husband, Ignacio. This was good because Ignacio and I could ride to work together.

Chapter 48

I returned to Mexicali, once more, got our furniture out of storage and with help from Ignacio and a friend, Isabel and I moved into the house. We were excited and settled nicely into our new home and awaited the arrival of our baby. The house was painted white on the outside with green trim and had a little yard with a little picket fence. Isabel was delighted and told me the house was just what she had pictured and hoped for. There was even room in our yard and garage to resume some of my art projects in my spare time. These projects were good therapy for me; I loved to spend time doing art and sculpting projects. After organizing things so I could work in the space, I began to plan what I would tackle. I had seen some large pots in a landscaping magazine that I wanted to try and had some ideas for sculpting some stone pieces similar to the ones I did in Acapulco years before.

Isabel and her sister started making the house a home, putting little touches that women do, like curtains and knick-knacks and such. Soon, the living room was painted a pleasing green, to match the different shades of green in the rest of the house. The windows let a lot of light in.

Despite all this, I really missed Mexicali. The new job was hard, grueling work and it was hot. It didn't offer much mental challenge, either. Promises to myself that I would find something better in time helped. I was used to mental challenges as Chief of Police, but I was determined to make the best of our move. I wanted Isabel to be happy.

L.A. was such a big town and the smog was thick even then. Learning to deal with the traffic and trying to get used to driving in such a town was hard but soon became easier as I got my bearings and knew the main highways and short cuts to our neighborhood.

Isabel was happy there and so excited about the baby. She and her sister had the nursery all ready and Isabel's mother planned to come and stay for a week as soon as the baby was born.

Right on time on a Sunday morning, within two days of her due date, Isabel told me breathlessly that she was in labor. I think it scared her when she had the first real pains. We had her bag ready and off we went to the hospital. They admitted her and put her in a room and sent me to the waiting room. Because, years ago, my first baby didn't live, I was extremely concerned about Isabel and our baby. In the waiting room I realized I had been pacing the floor when one of the nurses came by and said, "Don't worry, Mr. Velasquez, your wife is doing fine."

"Thank you," I answered, and sat down. Some magazines were scattered about so I picked one up and tried to concentrate, but couldn't. I hadn't eaten, but was too upset to think of food. I didn't let on at all, obviously, when they let me spend a few minutes with Isabel a couple times during her labor. I was cheerful and reassuring to my wife. I smiled, kissed her and patted her shoulder and told her everything would be fine. But, when back in the waiting room, my pacing began again. The nurse at the desk said, "Why don't you go down to the cafeteria and get a cup of coffee and a bite to eat, you'll feel better and honestly, the nurse in the labor room just told me that your wife is progressing normally and is just fine.

By this time I was tired and bored with sitting in the waiting room and I said, "Thank you, I think I will go down and get something. You'll know where I am if the Doctor comes out looking for me."

"Yes sir, we would have you paged immediately. Don't worry."

The coffee was good and I had a bowl of soup and a few crackers, read a newspaper and relaxed a little bit. Then I went back upstairs and finally, six hours after Isabel was admitted, the Doctor walked into the waiting room with a baby wrapped tight in a pink blanket with a little pink hat on her tiny head and said, "Congratulations Manuel, here is your baby daughter."

She was adorable, all pink with black hair and a little rosebud mouth. "Is Isabel all right?" I asked.

"Oh yes, you can take the baby in and visit for awhile, then Isabel needs to rest."

Isabel held out her arms for the baby as soon as I entered the room. She was smiling and her eyes were bright when she said, "Look how beautiful she is!"

"Well, of course Isabel, Emilia looks just like you," I said as I bent down and kissed my wife's forehead. We had decided months before that if we had a girl, we would name her Emilia. After we talked a few minutes more, the nurse came in again and told me that I should probably let Isabel have time to rest and return that evening at visiting hours.

Tiredness and relief were my feelings as I drove home and crashed on the couch.

That evening I visited mom and baby again and everything went well for the next couple days. Then on the third day, the Dr. released Isabel and the baby and I brought them home. It was a special time. Isabel had everything in the nursery ready for the baby and her mother was due to arrive and help out the next day. It was a happy home, grandma was a big help with the baby and Isabel got a needed rest. I was happy because Isabel and my new baby were fine.

Chapter 49

The job was tough for my brother-in-law, Ignacio and I. We were working on skyscraper construction. The foreman was very demanding all day, hardly letting us take time to wolf down a sandwich for lunch, let alone ever take a break. To make matters worse, the job started requiring overtime and I was beat at the end of a regular day. I wanted to go home to my family, have a good home cooked meal and maybe do a little of my art work in my spare time.

I didn't complain but Isabel knew I was struggling with both the difficulty of the job and the extra hours.

When little Emilia was about six months old, Isabel told me one evening at dinner that she was going to look for a job. "How can you do that? I asked her. We have a tiny baby." She quickly answered, "It's no use Manuel, I've already talked to my sister in law; she loves Emilia and can use the extra money so she's going to babysit. It will be fine. I need to get a job that has room for advancement and a decent wage and maybe even some insurance. You are working so hard I want to help financially too. We don't know what the future will bring. We could have a nest egg this way, maybe save a little money for a change. You gave up your job and made this move for me and now I want to help out."

"Well, Isabel, you seem to have your mind made up but we'll see how it goes. If it doesn't work well for us, you can always quit. The baby still gets you up at night, you may be too tired."

"Don't worry, I'll be fine." Isabel said softy to me as she came up behind me and put her arms around my neck.

Unlike my old macho self, I didn't protest any more. I instantly thought, "Well, if she wants to help out, why don't 'I just let her."

Two weeks later Isabel landed a job at the sheriff's department which was only about 12 miles away. Since I rode with Ignacio, I paid him extra for gas and Isabel was able to use our car to take Emilia to her sisters and to work and back.

Time went fast and Isabel settled into her job. I continued my job and fortunately Ignacio and I didn't have to work as many overtime hours. An announcement on the bulletin board at work told of an amnesty program being offered for Hispanics. I got the papers, filled them out and already had my green card so was granted U.S. citizenship.

Emilia was a year and a half old, toddling all around. Isabel handled everything fine, but once in awhile she either asked me to take Emilia to the park or somewhere so she could have some free time to either do house work or have coffee with a friend. Other times she would just say, "Honey, Emilia is going to be napping and I think I'll rest too, why don't you go have a beer with Ignacio and relax. We'll have a nice dinner later."

One Saturday Isabel told me she had a lot to do in the house and asked me to take Emilia for an outing.

My little daughter and I enjoyed the park nearby. I turned the little merry-go-round until she squealed and ran laughing, to the swings, then I pushed her in little swing and next put her on her favorite, the little fort with a swinging bridge for tiny kids. The outing wouldn't be complete without our stop at the ice cream parlor. Emilia loved her kid cone and I put a bib on her so she didn't get ice cream all over her outfit.

When we returned home that afternoon Isabel had left the house and there was a note lying on the drain board for me saying, "I've gone to do a few errands and I'll be back later."

I thought it was a little odd that she told me to take Emilia and leave so she could do chores at home and then left.

In the months that followed, Isabel was gone at odd times saying she had errands. She was late getting coming home from work a couple times and late from shopping.

I started to become suspicious that perhaps she had met someone at work and was actually seeing him. The reason I wondered about this was that Emilia was usually left with our sister in law and I couldn't see why Isabel couldn't have taken the baby with her to do errands. But she didn't. Sometimes she asked me to care for the baby while she went out, saying it was too hard to deal with a baby and do the necessary shopping.

One Saturday I decided to go have coffee with my cousin Roberto, who now lived in L.A. I was unhappy and wanted to talk to someone and he suggested a little cafe in the neighborhood. We met and had lunch. The food was good and reasonably priced. I especially liked the homemade pie with ice cream. Going for pie and coffee was my favorite outing. It was good to visit, we had been close for years.

A pretty waitress took our order and I couldn't resist teasing her a bit. She was kind of cool though and I think she thought I was arrogant. Isabel always told me to curb my teasing and not be so macho, because women don't find it attractive. I did learn to tone it down. Isabel actually had complimented me on my efforts.

One evening after Isabel came home late, I met her at the door and said, "If I find out that you are seeing someone, I won't put up with it and we will be done."

She answered, "Oh, Manuel, I went out for a beer with some girl friends and time just got away from me."

I said, "Well you've been late a lot lately. Have you met someone?"

She walked over to me, put her hand on my shoulder and said, "Oh, of course not, why would you even think that?" So I dropped it. I didn't want to make her miserable, but I still felt that something wasn't right.

Then came that awful night, about three weeks later, when Isabel came home late on a Friday and said, "I might as well tell you, I have met another man. I'm really, really sorry. I'm going to leave you. I just never thought this would happen. I have fallen very much in love with him." Isabel was sobbing as she continued, "I hope that you can somehow understand and that you won't hate me.

I was nearly blind with fury, I was always the one who left relationships or faded out of them until the woman ended it. This was the first time that I had been dumped and the tragedy was that Isabel was the love of my life. The hurt was real. We made the move to L. A. for her and I quit a job that I loved for her. I was absolutely undone.

When I tried to think of what to say, I was too upset to talk.

I finally answered, "I'm leaving the house tonight. I can't talk now." I threw some things in a bag and took off. I got a room nearby so that I could still ride to work with my brother-in-law. I knew I couldn't lose my job. With three kids to support, my path was set.

I lost my appetite and had trouble sleeping but knew I had to get over this anger and despair. My pride kept me from trying to win Isabel back and although I couldn't bear being around her, I had my sister in law help me work out visits with my baby daughter, Emilia.

Chapter 50

My cousin had noticed a small apartment for rent close to his and I moved out of the room I had rented (which was a board and room situation) into the apartment. There was more room and I would be able to do some cooking and make my lunches. The apartment was plain but fine for me at the time. Having my cousin close was good, too.

Roberto was so good to me at the time. He let me vent and listened patiently. We enjoyed visiting about our work and whether we should move back to Mexico or not and talked of having our own auto repair business someday. He was tall and fairly husky with his black hair combed straight back and a full moustache. He had not married. Roberto had a girlfriend for years and they always planned on marrying but before that happened, they drifted apart.

When he wasn't working, he dressed in western cut slacks, western style shirts with embroidered detail, cowboy hat and boots. He was a mechanic and had found good jobs in L.A.

Dancing was one of his favorite pastimes and on weekends he didn't have any trouble finding dance partners. Young women even called him on the phone asking him if he would be at a certain dance that weekend. I always teased him about his many admiring females.

Roberto and I routinely went back to that same restaurant and the same waitress waited on us. Her name was Celia and I found her very attractive and after several visits to the restaurant, she started to be a little more interested in my teasing her and my admiring compliments. After several months, I told my cousin that I thought Celia was absolutely gorgeous and spirited too. Roberto offered: "My friend owns this restaurant and told me she's single."

I replied, "Well you know I'm still not over Isabel, but what am I supposed to do? She's made it clear that we're done."

Sometime later, my cousin and I met at the restaurant and I was telling him that my divorce was almost final. I didn't realize that Celia was standing behind me and heard what I said. She came around to refill our coffee and said, "Forgive me, I heard you say your divorce would be final soon. I thought you were married but then you flirted a little and that made me wonder."

I looked at her, "It appears that I am going to be single very soon. I would love to take you to dinner some night, Celia."

She said, "Well, when you are officially single, I'd be delighted to go to dinner with you."

After the divorce was obtained, I went to the restaurant and told Celia that I was "officially single" and asked her for a date. She said, "Yes", and we made plans for the following Friday night.

I told Celia that we were going to have a casual, relaxing evening. I asked her if pizza and beer sounded good, then perhaps a drive to the beach. She said that sounded great.

She was so attractive, but I had only seen her in her waitress uniform. When I picked her up, she answered the door and I was surprised at how really beautiful she was. She had on a low cut blue blouse, a pair of well fitting jeans and scandals. She was fine featured, had medium length dark hair, beautiful eyes and her figure luscious.

The thought actually ran through my head at that moment that this would be the woman that I would love for the rest of my life, if she would have me. Who knows why love and attraction are sudden in some relationships and other times like this when I also felt more, like the old saying, "We were meant for each other".

I, of course, did not share this thought with her at the time but the premonition was strong. The feeling was in my heart. Something about her was peaceful and comforting to me. After the hurtful wounds from my relationship with Isabel, it was strange that my feelings toward Celia were so strong and that I didn't seem to have any doubt. This was before I had any idea that she would find me attractive or want me at all.

Everything was so easy and relaxing with Celia, we went to a popular pizza joint, had a couple beers each and got to know each other a little better. We shared with each other our past relationships, marriages, etc. Celia was 15 years younger than I, and had been married once. She had no children. I didn't elaborate on my prior marriages but did share with her that I had two boys and a girl. She was ecstatic. "I love children, she said, and would love to meet yours."

"That would be fine with me, I hope to have my boys up from Mexico for at least part of the summer and we could go on a picnic. "Perfect!" Celia said.

We drove toward the beach after leaving the pizza place and Celia scooted quite close to me in the front of the pickup. I put my arm around her and we had a relaxing drive, stopped and walked on the beach, shared a few warm kisses and embraces.

I was suffering a wounded ego and Celia quickly restored it by treating me very well and appreciating me by complimenting me often.

After about six months, Celia invited me to move in. She said she would welcome my company and that we could both save money by sharing expenses. We had talked of marriage but neither seemed ready to make that decision right then. Our relationship worked well, though, and it was like we were soul mates. No power struggles or bad tempers for us, we just seemed to think alike and agree even on things we had never taken time to discuss. There was no lack of passion in our love affair either. We were good together in every way.

Celia and Isabel met because of my visitations with my sweet daughter Emilia and since Isabel worked outside the home, she readily accepted Celia's offer to care for Emilia whenever Celia and I could help out. Over time, Celia was as much a mother to Emilia as Isabel. The two women worked everything out between them, were respectful and became friends too. This was really fortunate for all concerned. My boys spent time with us in the summer and Celia loved them.

Chapter 51

I was still working in construction and when our big project finished, there was a short lay off. One of the guys I worked with told me about some property he owned in a small community in the Mojave Desert. He was anxious to sell or lease/option it because he and his wife were moving away. I decided that I should take Celia to look at the place.

There were two acres and a mobile home. I fell in love with it. Celia liked it too. We both loved animals and were excited to have room for a couple of horses and maybe goats and rabbits. She wanted to have both flower gardens and a vegetable garden. I looked around and thought how great it would be to have room enough for all the projects I wanted to do. Never had I had enough room to store the expensive stone used for sculpting or the lumber, sacks of cement and rocks needed for garden statues. This was to be our own place and we discussed how we were going to offer the seller a lease with purchase option and exercise that option and if we were lucky and the seller agreed to these terms, we would own our own place eventually. We were so excited we could hardly sleep. The following day, we approached the seller with a lease-option to purchase which he readily accepted. Celia gave her 30 day notice of leaving to her landlord and we were able to move to the desert.

Celia had helped me with some art projects at her house. She liked helping me and did everything exactly as I asked her. She was good with all the tools and learned to anticipate what was needed before I ever had to ask. Once in awhile she tried something on her own and I applauded her efforts.

There was plenty of room to do my welded iron art and the other large sculpting projects as well as my newest project, the big decorative pots I had found a market for. First I made forms for these huge pots in three styles. After thinking for some time about finding a way to make really large pots that were reinforced, I experimented and developed a method. The pots had to be more rugged than smaller pots and not break easily. I used terracotta (clay) and added poly resin for strength. Then I poured the mixture into the molds. The pots were amazingly durable. For this reason I could make them as large as I wanted.

Hopefully, my customers would come out to the desert. I imagined they would enjoy the escape from the city and would remain loyal.

When not working on the art projects, I dabbled in swap meets, buying and selling things. I looked for odd things that I could incorporate into my large sculptures and also specialized in tack for horses with silver adornments. These were usually worth much more than I paid. So after I cleaned, repaired and refurbished them they were sold at a nice profit. I kept an ad in the paper for buying and selling this type of finery. Celia looked for old quilts she could restore and/or repair and sell at a good profit and she also advertised. In addition, she was always hunting for garden art pieces such as old benches, chairs, and unusual bird houses. She was good at repairing, restoring and selling them at a nice profit.

Chapter 52

The desert with the different flora, like red ocotillo, teddy bear cactus with yellow blossoms and purple grasses of the desert had to be captured with oil on my large canvases. These were about six feet by eight feet and sold well.

A landscaping company had also begun buying my sculptures and huge pots so I hoped I could make a living on the two acres.

About six months after we moved in, one of my customers brought a friend out to see our wares. She was the owner of an art gallery in L.A. with a good customer base. She was impressed with my art work and talked me into displaying some of my creations in a special showing. Included were the oil paintings, large sculptures and very large pots. Almost all the pieces sold. Several customers placed custom orders for colors and sizes they wanted.

That weekend Celia and I celebrated with a trip to the city. She had been instrumental in this success too. The quantity of pieces couldn't have been produced without her assistance. We booked a nice hotel in L.A., checked in and got ready for an evening on the town. Celia looked stunning in a low cut red dress and heels. I didn't know she had such a dress but was glad. We went out to a nice steak house and enjoyed a few drinks and a great dinner. Then as we were sipping after dinner drinks, I put my drink down, got down on one knee and told her I loved her and asked if she would marry me. A beautiful diamond ring I had bought for the occasion was dazzling in the open gold box in the palm of my hand. With tears coming down her cheeks, she pulled me to her and kissed me. It was a definite yes. She said she wanted to think about the plans for the wedding and enlist her sister's help and I said, anything you want is fine with me but I would prefer a smaller, more intimate affair with only family and close friends. We agreed that she needed some time to make the necessary choices and decisions so she wouldn't feel so stressed about the wedding. She deserved to be able to enjoy her wedding day.

Our marriage took place in a quaint little church just outside of Palermo, with our family and close friends attending. Celia and her sister planned everything. Celia wore her sister's wedding dress. She looked stunning in the white lace dress and a headpiece of yellow, purple and red flowers. The church was decorated with more of the brightly colored blossoms. I rented a black tux with a white jacket and Celia told me I took her breath away. She had a way of making me feel special. Her sister was her maid of honor and my brother-in-law Bob, was my best man. At a small Mexican fiesta in the reception hall adjoining the church, we danced and sang and began marriage on a happy note. A honeymoon was out of the question because we hadn't the time. Orders from the recent show at the gallery had to be done.

Chapter 53

Ten months later Celia gave birth to our first son, Francisco. We were pleased, especially Celia, because this was her first child. When my boys visited that summer they adored the baby. They had room to run and play and rode the horse on paths nearby every day.

I kept busy with orders coming in after the art gallery showing and Celia helped me when she could and worked on her projects too while taking care of our new baby. She was wonderful to my boys too and they loved her. We still had my daughter Emilia with us much of the time.

Soon after, a well known builder made a visit to see my landscaping pieces. Fortunately, he liked my work and told me the items were unusual and that he would send some business my way. He built unusual custom homes that looked natural in the desert and gave my business cards to his clients. Owners of these homes were able to pay me well and enjoyed one of a kind sculptures and unusually decorated large pots in their yards.

After thinking for years about making lamps, I designed three of wrought iron.

Having the time and room to pursue my craft was so good for me. I felt I had a ton of energy and worked late into the night many times on this project. After sketching them in detail, I welded and sculpted the wrought iron into the design. The electric lamp fixture was added last. All along my plan was to finish them, show them to lamp companies and hopefully take orders for these custom built lamps.

Friends and family encouraged me, and told me the lamps were unusual. First I went to Inland Lighting Co. and showed the lamps to them. Luck was with me that day. They liked them and immediately added the three designs to their custom division. I was to do as many as I could for them in the next month. I made the lamps and delivered them to Inland and they paid me a good price.

Inland promised they would give me royalties for my designs. They planned to mass produce them later. Their book-keeper was to send the paperwork out to me. Unfortunately, I never received it. I didn't even think at that time to hire an attorney because I couldn't imagine that this big company would short me my royalties. Life was going by and Celia and I were busy all the time. Inland bought the lamps as I made them and we needed the extra money.

Chapter 54

Even though we loved the two acres and the desert, my customers just didn't seem willing to come that far to buy my artwork. It was also a long drive to town when I had to meet with them or deliver orders.

We had been in the desert two years when I got a phone call one morning from Mexicali offering me the position back. The timing was perfect. I knew I wanted to move back to Mexicali. We would be closer to my boys and I was ready to return to law enforcement and detective work. I asked Celia if she would be alright with that and she said, "Of course."

I made decisions fast and Celia was always willing to go wherever I wished and be a good help mate.

We made preparations to move right away. First we contacted the seller of the home and two acres and advised him that we were moving and to re-list the property. I went to Inland and told them I wouldn't be making the custom lamps and that they could begin their production. I asked them if they would check on my receiving royalties and they advised me that they would look into it. They never addressed my inquiries and I never received royalties. Twenty years later, the three styles I designed were still included in the inventory of lamps at Inland Lighting.

I went ahead to Mexicali and rented a comfortable home close to the police station and returned three days later to California. Celia and I packed our necessary belongings then sold everything else at our yard sale. Then with little Francisco on his mother's lap, and towing a full utility trailer behind the pickup, we headed off to Mexico.

How great it was to be back in Mexicali. I settled right into my old job. Most of the people I worked with before were still there. Several of my friends were still working close by and we had coffee together. Celia and Francisco settled right in. They liked the home and seemed to like the town. Best of all, they all made good friends right away.

Celia got pregnant again and decided to return to Palermo to have her OB/GYN specialist deliver the baby because she had confidence in him. She thought it would be wise to have the child born in the United States too. Our son Gilberto was born a year after we moved to Mexicali. I drove Celia to Palermo when she was near her due date. All went well. He was a happy baby and Francisco was delighted with his new brother.

Work was busy and exciting. All kinds of police calls came in as you would expect. The months went by, and then stretched into three years.

Chapter 55

The phone rang one evening and it was my mother, crying, asking if she could come and live with us, that she had no other means of support and had lost her home because she had fallen ill and couldn't pay the mortgage. This was a huge surprise to me as my mother and I had been estranged for some years. I told her I needed to discuss the matter with Celia and that I would call her back. Celia was gracious and said she thought it may be good for my mother and I to finally make amends. I called mom back and told her to come ahead. My brother and sister were to help her pack up her few necessary belongings, store the rest at their home and bring mom to Mexicali.

Unfortunately, things didn't go well with mom. She was sullen and I felt she was trying to make trouble between Celia and me. She was getting well though so we felt we had done the right thing letting her move in.

Celia and I took off in the car one Saturday. Our favorite outing was to drive to the bus station and then take the bus downtown. Breakfast was always shared at "Rosita's". Then we shopped some, picked out some special candy or pastry. Most important though were special toys or games for the boys. Not expensive but chosen with care. Celia, of course, perused the ladies' clothing, jewelry, makeup and shoes while I sat outside the store relaxing, sipping a soda in the shade. Then it was my turn. Yes, to the sporting goods store we went. I mainly wanted to look at guns, ammo and outdoor stuff but resisted purchasing any. A stop for art supplies for my current project completed our shopping. I was doing the large canvases of the desert again and needed the oil paints. Sitting across the aisle from me on the return bus trip was Linda, a lady we knew. She asked if we could drive her to the "Curandero" (healer) on the way home. I told her we'd be glad to help. Linda explained that the healer would cleanse her body of any witchcraft that anyone was doing or had done to her. The healer charged for the service but modestly. It sounded kind of interesting.

Celia and I went along and after introductions sat reading magazines while we waited. There was a pitcher of ice water and glasses so we helped ourselves.

The healer lived in a nondescript bungalow and had a small waiting room in the front of the home with an office adjoining.

When Linda returned to the waiting room, the healer came in and immediately looked right into my eyes without wavering and said, "Manuel, please come in for a visit with me, I strongly sense that you need my help." Oh, I'm sorry, I replied, I've never been into this type thing and don't really think I want to."

"This first visit will be free," she said quickly. "I have time for you and detect possible problems. You may be a victim of witchcraft. I can help. Celia should be checked out also. I would like to talk to you and your wife. Let me do this, you may think differently after I'm done."

I was completely surprised but she was so adamant about it that I answered, "Well alright, if you think it's necessary", and we followed her into her office while Linda waited.

When we were seated, she said, "There is someone close to you that I detect has been doing witchcraft on you for a time now maybe intermittently. Share with me your background a little and current situation. How has your family's health been lately? How is your marriage? I was at a loss to answer but Celia answered right away, "Manuel's mother has been living with us for about a year and she's really different. She has been mean to Manuel in his childhood and kicked his father out of the house after he became ill. Since she's been with us, things haven't gone well."

I added, "Our once perfect marriage has been deteriorating. We have had some arguments and disagreements that are unusual for us. Usually we agree on most things but not lately." Then I told her about a mysterious flu like illness that we and the boys had suffered about a month prior.

"Manuel," she asked, "Think back. Did your father become ill gradually before your mom kicked him out of the house?"

"As a matter of fact, yes, my brother, sister and I couldn't figure out what was wrong with him. We felt so bad for him. He's better now and he and I are very close."

"Alright, the healer stated, the illness unless otherwise explained, was probably witchcraft done by your mom. Celia said, "One day your mom actually hinted at feeling guilty at something she had done that caused your dad to be sick, but when

I asked about it, she clammed up and wouldn't tell me anything else.

My feelings tell me it is someone very close to you doing some witchcraft on you Manuel. Has your young life been normal or have you had trials and tragedies?"

"Well, I answered, my mother never seemed to love me. She yelled at me, beat me, and never had a kind word for me. She found fault continually with every-thing I said or did, even though I even missed school to watch the younger children and help her. Then I married young and moved out of the family home. Our first child was stillborn however.

My marriages were wrought with problems. This is my third marriage. In the military I did defy death more than once though, but I was far away from mom at the time.

The healer stood up and said, "I strongly recommend that you remove your mother from your home." Her voice even louder, she pointed to me and continued: "It is of utmost importance that she no longer has access to your home and family."

I leaned forward in my chair to hear more. When the healer finished talking,

Celia was nodded in agreement and said, "She's right".

After your mother has gone, you will begin to heal and I would like to work with you both a little to make sure the spells are broken. You will no doubt find strange things around your home. There will probably be bundles of dirt, feathers, sticks with chicken blood on them tied with string and all manner of odd things. These must all be removed and burned.

I called my siblings the next day and told them mom couldn't stay with us any longer. Fortunately my sister had a good job at the time and offered to have mom stay with her in her apartment. I warned my sister but she said mom wouldn't perform witchcraft on her. I had her call mom and invite her. Since sis lived close to town, mom was happy to move.

Once mom was out of the house permanently, we began our search for odd items like the healer described. It was shocking how many of these different bundles and similar things we found. They were stashed everywhere. We found bundles just as the healer described and even loose dirt and dried chicken feet in a couple dresser drawers, high in the closets, behind furniture and in the garage hidden on shelves behind things. As instructed, we burned everything we found in a burn barrel in the vacant lot nearby.

We reported our findings to the healer and both visited her routinely to make sure we were out from under any spells. We took the boys to her once also. Soon we began to get along better, our marriage improved in every way. The boys settled down, seemed much calmer and the pink returned to their cheeks. They stopped their mean fighting too.

Celia had caught them terrorizing a cat a few months before and thought it was so out of character for them. Now they were peaceful loving boys again

Things were quite normal and work was busy. Time went by fast. The boys kept us hopping with activities and play.

Chapter 56

One evening after I got home from work, Celia asked how my day went. I walked over to where she was working at the drain board in the kitchen, put my arms around her and gave her a big hug, and told her "Just had one bad case we're investigating where two men were shot at a big dog fighting event."

"Tell me all about it Manuel, what is going on?"

"Let's enjoy our evening sweetie, and later I'll share the particulars of the case. It will be in the newspaper anyway."

The boys were still up, running around the house, and I didn't want to share the criminal elements with Celia right then. Later that night I told her what had happened in the case.

A fight had broken out quickly among the big money gamblers at the dog fights and a man pulled a gun and shot two men who he believed were going to kill him. The reason was money, and a lot of it. In the dog fighting culture there is heavy betting and trouble follows. This investigation didn't take long because there were several witnesses who identified the shooter.

Dog fighting is a serious concern because the dog handlers are often involved in illegal gambling and sale and possession of illegal weapons. Unfortunately it is not uncommon for dog handlers or spectators to involve their children in the whole activity from beginning to end. About all enforcement officers and concerned citizens can do is make others aware of the realities of the sport. Like cock fighting, dog fighting has been popular for generations. It is still legal and regulated in other countries. However, the law preventing cruelty to animals, enacted in President Bush's term, has helped eradicate the activity here.

Within the last couple years, large busts have taken place here in the states. One such bust in West Palm Beach Florida resulted in 60 arrests, confiscation of 12 dogs and $89,000 in cash. Seized also were drugs with a value of $50,000.

In the United States, especially New Orleans, North Carolina and New York, prize pit bulls have been raised for generations. Some of these dogs' blood lines are known around the world. The owners breed their animals every six months. The puppies bring $1500 to $2,000 each. Prize pit bulls raised by successful breeders often bring $8,000 to $10,000 for the pick of the litter. After they have proven themselves, a successful fighting dog, can be worth $25,000.

There are always crimes associated with dog and rooster fighting. One surprising case involved a directional mine being placed on the road into the property of a man who held dog fights. If anyone came around that wasn't supposed to, they wouldn't know about the mine and it would go off. The mine was full of pellets. A land surveyor was shot, though not seriously, by one of these mines, and that's how the authorities learned of the mine use.

Chapter 57

Work was busy with the usual things. Then one fateful afternoon a call came through our emergency line that somebody was burglarizing a house. One of our officers was following the perpetrator who was trying to escape with stolen goods. The officer asked for backup and my partner and I responded instantly. We jumped in my pickup and sped to the scene.

The thief was pulling a makeshift wagon with gunny sacks full of loot in them. The officer shouted, "Halt this is the law and I'm armed." The thief started running away trying to pull the wagon and actually took a shot at the officer. He then went up an alley that was too narrow for us to drive in the pickup. We continued on foot at a dead run to chase this bizarre criminal. Risking being shot for the value of the items he took was crazy. I sent my partner back after the pickup as we were neared a road. He met us as we came out of the alley and I jumped in the back of the pickup. As the thief ran ahead into the street, he kept shooting; we carefully returned fire. We had to be mindful of stray bullets in a neighborhood like this. A bullet grazed him in the thigh but he kept moving. The thief took a couple more shots at us that missed and we shot back. Although bleeding now, the injured man was dodging left and right, still running and pulling the wagon. I saw my bullets hit the dirt and my partners also fell short too. By this time the burglar was tiring.

As trained professionals, we were careful with weaponry. Unfortunately, the thief was not. A stray bullet from his gun ricocheted and hit a lady that was standing up on the balcony of her house. She was just standing there, seemed fine and it appeared the bullet grazed her arm. A bystander shouted, "She's been shot," and pointed to the lady on the balcony.

As we drove by, we stopped briefly. I jumped out, ran up the few stairs to her balcony and asked the woman if she was alright. She said, "Yes, I think so."

I said, "Miss, stay still. Help is on the way, we radioed ahead for an ambulance."

In pursuit of the thief, we pressed on. Soon we apprehended him. There were two bullet holes in the truck where he had fired at us.

Our thief had lost some blood and his wound needed attention so we took him to the hospital for treatment. Returning to the station, the bandit was booked quickly into jail. He loudly stated to the crowd that gathered: "If I get out of jail I'm going to put a *savanaso* on Manuel Velasquez. He knew me by name although I did not recognize him. (A *savanaso* is where a group of people wearing sheets cover the head of a victim and punch with an ice pick). I was actually worried about his threat, about the whole thing; this guy was crazy enough to do most anything.

In the two big gunnysacks were a willy-nilly array of items including hand tools from the shed, all the couples' jewelry, (he didn't take time to pick and choose), and money that the lady of the house had stashed in a cookie jar on the drain board. In addition there was a set of silver goblets, a collection of Remington brass figurines, as well as a radio and brand new camera. Also there were other odds and ends he just threw in the sacks hastily.

Chapter 58

I was sitting in my office late that afternoon filling out my report when my boss came in, closed the door behind him and said, "You need to tell me how all this came down today."

"Of course", I answered.

He sank into a chair, wiped his furrowed brow and announced, "Someone said a lady standing on her balcony was shot in this foray today?"

I began relating the entire episode to my boss in detail and just as I finished, an officer ran into the office and said, "That lady on the balcony died that was shot in the chase."

I felt sick hearing the news; she had been standing there when I talked to her, with a small wound on her arm. The doctor said that evidently the bullet grazed her arm and went clear through her body. I can still remember her standing there, a pretty middle aged woman.

My boss immediately informed me that as soon as we gave our statements my partner and I were to go to our homes and stay put. We gave our sworn statements, the names of witnesses that observed the chase, and then went directly to our homes to wait for further instructions. An investigation had to be done immediately and since we were involved, we had to give them time to sort it all out.

Returning home, I told Celia of the tragedy. She talked to me and tried to comfort me. Mulling it over and over in my mind, I knew it was the thief's bullet as he was shooting carelessly. It was a terrible thing and so unnecessary.

"Were we somehow responsible?" I asked myself as I thought over the events of the day. I had trouble sleeping for weeks because of her death. "What should we have done different?" In hindsight, it seemed we would have been better off to let the thief go, had we any idea a life would be lost.

After years of a flawless career, this tragedy was also embarrassing. Here we were instructed to stay at home. As the days went by, I resented it and thought it was taking too much time to conduct the investigation.

Then a week later, according to my boss, some lawyers from Mexico City arrived and kept asking more and more questions of the witnesses. He received instructions from someone, called me in after hours one evening and said, "Someone very high up wants to pin this shooting on you. He then told me that he was supposed to detain me but he said, "You didn't hear this from me." I'm telling you, Manuel, this doesn't look good," You will be put in jail soon, and they'll hold you and somehow frame you with this shooting. This must date back to enemies from your military career. You better get out of town as fast as you can. I will do nothing for 24 hours, that's all the time I can give you. After that if you are still here, I will have to arrest you if I'm ordered to do so. I know you are experienced and it wasn't your bullet. This is so unfair and you don't know how much I'll miss you.

He told me he would do me one last favor. He promised to make entries in my file after a couple days that I had been spotted in Buenos Aires, Argentina, by a couple different sources. He knew me and knew I was innocent. Goodbye Manuel and good luck," He said as he took me by the shoulder and steered me toward the door.

"Thanks so much for everything sir, I'll miss you too," I said quietly to him as I left.

What a jolt! And to make matters worse, I needed paperwork to return to the

U.S. fast. I rushed to a forger's hangout. I knew he could prepare false identification and the papers I needed to go back into the U.S. I hadn't been asked to relinquish my papers used to travel in and out of the U.S. but figured they would nab me at the border if my real name was used. Celia was at home with our little boys. They could travel back to the states easily as they were U.S. citizens. We threw the necessary things together and in the dead of night left Mexicali.

Chapter 59

Stopping only for necessities we headed to Wenatchee, Washington. Celia's sister and her husband lived there and we knew we could stay with them for awhile. No one in Mexicali knew Celia's family ties. They were very gracious and we rested up from the long trip. The trauma of the situation we left behind weighed heavily on our minds. For me it was a nightmare. I loved my job in Mexicali and the people I worked with. My reputation was excellent and I was a respected member of the community. My salary was good there too and I didn't know how I would support our family here. Feeling sad, I was also mulling over and over the fact that it would be difficult to see my older children. Washington was a lot farther than California and with a warrant out for me, I knew I would have to wait awhile to see them, but I would find a way.

Celia didn't realize the extent of my unhappiness because she was happy to be with her family and hadn't really lived in Mexicali long enough to feel like it had really been her home.

With the events that took place in Mexicali, I knew I would look over my shoulder for a very long time even though no one would probably locate me in Washington. Turning my name around, I switched my middle name, Monrovia to my last name, and then used Velasquez for my middle name.

I was able to land a job as an equipment maintenance person at a large fruit warehouse. I had gained experience on similar machinery at different jobs so I felt qualified. Getting a good job was the beginning of my accepting a new life, in a new place. Celia wanted to help out and was hired by a popular restaurant a few miles away as a waitress. She seemed to enjoy the people and the tips were good.

After we had both gotten jobs, we began house hunting. We soon located a roomy home in the country on two and a half acres with an oversized garage. Celia loved the house. It was modern and one of the nicest she'd ever lived in. The boys found the country suited their need to run free. They bicycled, fished and swam in the river and raised their exotic animals. Our animals were left with friends so we had to replace them. We kept iguanas, snakes, exotic jungle birds and the newest addition was a baby alligator, one of the fastest animals there is. My youngest son Gilberto learned to be faster and faster when he held a fish up to feed the gator because the gator became faster as it grew.

Captive alligators always seek freedom (in the neighborhood) and this one did.

A couple years after we moved there, a young man came to the door and said he was a reporter. He had learned of us through the man at the feed store. He asked if he could interview us about the animals and take pictures for an article in the local paper. The boys were excited so we did the interview and a half page story came out in the newspaper with good pictures of us with the animals.

I had art projects; my newest was welding end tables and coffee tables, ornate coat racks and more lamps. Some were burnished metal, some I painted different colors, mostly Tuscan colors which were popular. A decorating store, The Design Den bought almost all of them for a client that built a huge home overlooking the valley. I got excellent prices for the items and was encouraged and set about making more. The large desert oils and big landscaping pots sold well too.

Chapter 60

We met our neighbor Dorothy early on and became fast friends. She lived on the family farm alone. Soon Celia became like a daughter to her and I had become as close as her own son who lived in another town and wasn't able to help much. We visited and helped each other and shared our hopes and dreams. Dorothy could no longer do the repairs to the fences, cut or stack fire wood, or do any maintenance chores on the farm so I did these things for her. Celia and I helped her with everything on her 12 acre home place. Our landlord, Gary, was really good to us and loaned us enough for a down payment on some land. The problem was, it was undeveloped and we couldn't get a construction loan on it. We kept it though and made small monthly payments figuring it would be a good investment. Dorothy knew we wanted to build a house ourselves. One evening she suggested we work together for a common goal. She suggested an agreement that would serve both families' needs. She said that she would deed a two acre parcel to us and provide enough money to begin construction of a home. In return we were to care for Dorothy the remainder of her life. We talked about the arrangement and thoroughly discussed every situation we could think of that could arise. We reached an agreement and Dorothy had her attorney draw up the papers and deeded the property to us.

With a deed and help from Dorothy, we were able to do most of the construction.

We purchased a used fifth wheel trailer, moved it on the property and lived in it while we built the home in our spare time. Things went well, the boys and Celia helped and we even snuck away for camping and fishing some weekends. A year and a half later, we moved into our new home. It wasn't quite done but was livable. We had a party that weekend in celebration. At that time, since I figured the police were searching for me in Argentina, I arranged for my other children to come and visit several times and we all enjoyed being together. There was so much crime I hoped the police were kept busy just with their current work.

After the main construction of the house, I was able to use the big workshop, where we did the carpentry work, for my art projects. Things were still selling well and I loved the creative process. I changed the large oil paintings to local scenes. Since there were definite seasons, I painted the orchards in bloom in the spring and harvest scenes in the fall. Then I did a scene with a blanket of snow wrapping the trees in winter. Snow scenes were new to me and challenging. People liked them and bought them. The Design Den featured a couple in their store at all times for me on consignment.

Everything went well with our arrangement with Dorothy. We were all one big family. I was able to buy motorbikes; Celia and I took the kids to the mountains often to camp and play. I was given a promotion to day supervisor at work and liked my job. We were all busy and seven years went by quickly. By now, I didn't worry about a warrant, although once in awhile I thought of it and was glad that time had gone by without incident.

Chapter 61

Then I had some bouts of illness. I thought I may have developed an ulcer and when I saw my doctor, he agreed, but wanted to order a CAT scan. I declined, thinking I would be alright with the medicine the doctor ordered. Fortunately I rallied and did better at times. But during another onset of symptoms, I stayed in bed a lot and got up only for necessities. My son put a sturdy chair in the shower and the hose was long enough that I could manage my shower alone.

Joining the family at the table for dinner was the highlight of my day. Listening to their banter and laughter boosted my spirits for at least a short time.

Chapter 62

One morning I woke up late. Celia had been up early. I heard the morning sounds of coffee brewing, breakfast chatter as she fed the boys, then her loud instance that they get out to the bus stop before they missed the school bus. She came in with a tray and we visited a little. She was always attentive, worried that I would get lonesome. She said, "Honey, before you have your cereal and fruit, I want to try and old family remedy that may alleviate some of the pain you've been having and get some of the toxins out of your body."

"Oh Celia, you know I don't really believe most of these things but go ahead. Don't tell me it has something to do with those two eggs on that tray?"

"Yes, she laughed, but it will be painless. I'm simply going to pass them over your body, that's all."

"Well, this is superstition and no more," but I smiled weakly and said, "Go Ahead then."

She took one egg, made the sign of the cross over my forehead and did just as she said, passed it over my body, touching it lightly my skin. Then she did the same with the second egg. When she finished she took the two eggs over to the tray. She had two large glasses of water on the tray and she broke an egg into each. It was spooky because the entire liquid, eggs and water, turned almost black. Even though I did not believe in those old customs, I was really surprised. She said it was important that she dispose of the foul liquids outside in a hold in the ground and that she'd wash up and be right back with my breakfast.

By that afternoon I really had to admit to Celia that I did feel less pain and my energy level was better. At dinner, I actually joined in the conversation. Celia performed the egg therapy on me once a week.

Then I got a little better and would work some more and all was well. I was concerned because since I had missed so much work, my income was less. We forged on. I was able to keep my art project customers happy and they liked my work. The extra money was needed. We liked Wenatchee; the weather was nice and sunny, even in the winter.

My daughter Emelia spent time with us that summer and my older boys came for a visit too. The kids all got along well and it was a joy to watch them. They seemed happy and like children, didn't seem to have a worry in the world.

Chapter 63

Right after hearing an auto accident on the sharp curve close to my property one morning, I told Celia to call the sheriff and I went to lend assistance. I had helped many times in the past, often reaching the scene before the sheriff or ambulance arrived. Because of my training, I knew a lot about watching for symptoms of shock and administering first aid and medical treatment. Approaching the vehicle which had rolled and was sitting on its side in the ditch, I went around and made sure the driver was alright. He was by himself in the car and had a cut on his forehead that was bleeding. He complained of back and leg pain but was definitely trapped in the car. The doors had been damaged in the roll and looked like they may be hard to open. I talked to the driver and assured him help was on the way.

Soon Sheriff Gendron arrived and next the ambulance and crew pulled up, siren on and lights blaring. We had to remove the car door from its hinges so the paramedics and ambulance crew could get him out of the car and administer aid. Then the ambulance left and took the injured driver to the hospital.

I had helped many times before and became acquainted with Sheriff Gendron.

After the ordeal, the Sheriff said, "I was going to call you tomorrow Manuel, we need to talk." Well come on over to the house, we'll have ice tea, I answered. We washed our hands and sat down.

Sherriff Gendron was a tall, husky man. His red hair always looked like it was a week past time for a haircut. His moustache was also red and wide. His voice was deep and when he laughed it was like a small roar. We visited often. He would stop by when he was in the neighborhood and we'd swap stories and talk about our youth.

Celia poured ice tea in large glasses for us then brought a plate of cookies to the table. "Thanks Celia," Sheriff Gendron said. We talked about the wreck and whether the county would ever try to make the corner a bit safer. Then he looked down at the floor, hesitated before speaking, looked over at me, sighed and said, "I hate to give you this news, but we received a Federal Warrant a couple days ago directing us to apprehend you. I recognized your picture. The Mexican government states they want you extradited. Manuel, can you contact an attorney there and try to get this dropped? It looks like an old charge. "

I replied, "It is old and I'm surprised to hear this, can you give me a week at least? It will take some time to get help with this."

"Yes, of course, but not much longer I'm afraid."

That day, I called Seattle and made an appointment with an attorney specializing in Mexican-American matters. His immediate fee was $5,000. I had been ill off and on and didn't have the cash. Dorothy insisted on going along with Celia and me. She loaned me the $5,000 for the attorney. We all went in for the conference and the attorney read the warrant, studied parts of it again, leaned back in his chair and said, "I will request that your court file from Mexicali be rushed to me. Do you have an attorney there that would help?

I said, "No, but I have connections that will help me find one fast."

"Good, he said, get back to me then and I'll ask for an extension of thirty days on the warrant. I can usually get that much time up front." I thanked him and we left his office, I was worried about all this; the case was old, why were they even working it yet. Dorothy and Celia were both concerned too so I started being upbeat, told them not to worry and stopped at the mall so they could look around for awhile. We had plenty of time and they always loved to shop a bit. Later we had a little lunch, and then drove back to Wenatchee. It was a beautiful day with the sun shining on the snow covered mountain peaks, little waterfalls coming down off the lower hills and we enjoyed the day in spite of the circumstances.

Early the next morning I contacted a reputable attorney in Mexicali that was highly recommended by my prior partner there. My partner was a man I could trust and I didn't divulge where I was living. The attorney promised to investigate the file and warrant and report back to me.

Before he ever called back, I fell ill again. My doctor ordered a CT scan. He gave me a diagnosis of advanced stomach cancer. Based on my grave condition he estimated that I only had three weeks to live.

The irony of it all staggered me. I was only 55, had lived through countless death defying situations and now this. The warrant evidently would not be a problem now.

Every waking hour my energies went to set my affairs in order the best I could. I had to instruct Celia and the boys how to finish a few last minute repairs on the house. There were also a few routine maintenance chores I instructed them about too. Winterizing had to be done on our house and Dorothy's and I wanted to make sure they wouldn't forget.

The end was near, the pain great and how could I feel slighted? I lived more in my lifetime than most men could ever dream of.

Although I was concerned for my wife and sons and wished with all my heart that I could still be there with them, I was glad they had the security we had worked for. The home was paid for and the remainder of the land contract was being worked out by Celia's agreement to care for Dorothy the remainder of her life. Seven years had already passed during which we both cared for Dorothy. I told her how much I appreciated her helping us. She said, "Oh I have been so glad to have you all here, life would be so lonely without you, and thank you for everything you have done for me."

As the end draws near, I am not frightened in spite of my total lack of belief in a higher power or entity. I have been an atheist most of my life. Celia made me comfortable and my grown children were able to come visit me. Now, sick, tired and spent, I know I will soon draw my last breath.

EPILOGUE

Manuel passed away before a copy of his court file arrived in the mail from the attorney in Mexico.

President Luis Echeverria, who took office in 1970 and served until 1976, was formerly a law professor and a member of the ruling Institutional Revolutionary party. Echeverria had served as Interior Secretary from 1964-1970 and gained prominence for his stern handling of student demonstrations during the 1968 Olympic Games in Mexico City.

However, years went by and investigations continued and Echeverria was arrested in 2006 on genocide charges in connection with his role during the massacre of student protesters in Tlatelco in 1968. This change overturned a lower court ruling that the statute of limitations had run out. Echeverria was 84 at the time of these 2006 charges.

About the Author

Phyllis Owens

Most of the authors working life was spent as a paralegal and then division manager of a law firm. Prior to that she helped her husband Tom in their "Goldendale Ranch Meat Company" as a confidante, meat-wrapper, bookkeeper, errand girl and office manager.

After retiring she planned to write novels and short stories.

This story, is about a man who lived an interesting, unusual and dangerous life. The author felt it needed to be remembered.

Phyllis Owens lives in Yakima, Washington. She and her husband Tom have three children and four grandchildren. Family has always been important to them.

Contact the author at: tnpo@charter.net